CAPTIVE TREASURE

by Milly Howard

Bob Jones University Press, Greenville, South Carolina 29614

Captive Treasure

Edited by Mark Sidwell and Olivia Tschappler

Cover and illustrations by Cheryl L. Weikel

©1988 by Bob Jones University Press
Greenville, South Carolina 29614

ISBN 0-89084-440-2
Printed in the United States of America

20   19   18   17   16   15   14   13   12

To Jessica

And long, lazy afternoon naps

Publisher's Note

For Carrie Talbot, like many of today's Christian young people, God's Word is a part of her daily life. She memorizes verses with her preacher father and learns to read from the Bible at her mother's knee. She knows about the lessons that the Scripture teaches but has a difficult time putting into practice what she knows. When in trouble, she finds it just as easy to turn to her parents as to turn to the Lord.

Then, traveling west on a wagon train, Carrie is captured by the Indians. Without her parents to guide her, she has to rely totally on the Lord. Finally, when her Bible is stolen, she finds that her greatest treasure is the Scripture she has hidden in her heart.

As she witnesses for the Lord in the Indian camp, Carrie sees some seed fall by the wayside when Lone Wolf angrily rejects her words. Other seed falls on stony ground when the members of the tribe treat the gospel as no more than a good story. She sees the seed choked by thorns when Swift Arrow understands but does not wish to endanger his position in the tribe. Some seed does bear fruit, however, and Carrie sees the Keeper and Sky Woman come to know the Lord.

This is a story of great courage and stirring adventure, of spiritual growth and personal relationships with God. It is the story of a brave girl who learns to stand alone for God in difficult circumstances.

Contents

1   The Jumping-Off Point   1

2   Dusty Trails   13

3   Warrior's Moon   27

4   Lodgepoles by the River   37

5   The Medicine Bundle   49

6   Daughter of the Sun   61

7   Wolves of Hunger   71

8   The Challenge   83

9   Winter Winds   95

10 One Man's Treasure   107

11 Night Raid   119

12 The Sundance   131

13 The North Star   145

14 Home   157

    Author's Note   167

Chapter One

The Jumping-Off Point

"Saint Joe, dead ahead!"

The *River Queen*'s whistle shrilled, and her huge paddle wheels churned the water. Carrie Talbot ran back and forth on the crowded deck of the steamer. Nowhere could she find an empty place at the rail.

She tried climbing up on a keg so that she could see over the heads of the people. But tall hats and wide bonnets blocked everything except the bright blue of the summer sky. She tried scrunching down low to see between the rails. But tall boots and wide skirts blocked everything except the dirty brown of the river water.

Suddenly, strong hands clasped her around the waist and scooped her up. Her surprised shriek turned to laughter when she looked into her father's eyes. He took off his hat and swung her up to his broad shoulders. Carrie clutched at his head as her long legs dangled.

"You're not quite grown up yet, I see," he teased. "Hold on tight, now. I might drop you." He braced his feet on the deck. Carrie's brown eyes sparkled with excitement. She swung her coppery braids out of the way and leaned forward.

The steamer eased around the bend. A great shout rose from the watching passengers. "Saint Joe!"

"Saint Joe," Carrie repeated eagerly. "The jumping-off place!"

"And the first step West."

Carrie barely heard her mother's quiet voice, but she felt her father shift position. She glanced down and saw him put his free arm around his wife. Carrie wiggled down to stand with them. Dimly she realized that their excitement was as great as her own.

Another emigrant turned to smile at them. "I see you're as eager as the rest of us, Preacher."

Nathan Talbot nodded. "My brother wrote that I was needed," he replied. "He established a mission out West. The Lord has truly blessed his work with the Indians."

"I wish you well, then," the emigrant replied slowly. "Not all have fared as well with the Indians."

The man left to join his family at the rail. Martha Talbot stared after him. She reached for Carrie. Absent-mindedly she smoothed the fiery strands that refused to stay in Carrie's thick braids.

"Don't mind him, Ma," Carrie said cheerfully. "God will take care of us, just like He always has, right, Pa?"

A smile lit Mrs. Talbot's face as her husband's firm *amen* rolled over the noise of the crowd.

"I know, child," she said gently. She gave Carrie's hair one last pat and let her go.

The deck shuddered under their feet as the engine reversed. The crowd shifted. A space at the rail opened up. Carrie darted forward and squeezed in. She clutched the rail and stared at the busy wharf on the bank.

The wharf was crowded with goods and scurrying people. Empty supply wagons lined the bank above it. The drivers tried to quiet their restless mules as they waited to load their wagons. On the dock, waiting passengers got in the way of the dockhands. A few children clutched tightly to their mothers' hands. Others ran wildly about, shouting in excitement. Yelping dogs added their clamor to the shouts of the workers.

Another shuddering bump and the boat docked. The gangplank slowly creaked down. The crowd surged forward. Most of the passengers hurried across the wharf to the dirt road that led into the rough town of St. Joseph, Missouri.

Carrie shifted from one foot to the other as the folds of a full cape swept across her face. Impatience tugged at her. It urged her to join the crowd and hurry into the exciting bustle below. Common sense told her to stay put. For once, Carrie obeyed the voice of caution. She waited until the crowd thinned. Then she saw her mother waiting by the gangplank, a worried expression on her face.

"Here, Ma!" Carrie shouted.

The usual smile swept across her mother's face as Carrie hurried forward. "Carrie," she scolded lightly. "You could have been swept overboard!"

"Not the way she was holding on," Mr. Talbot said. "Not a moment's worry, Martha. We can count on Carrie to keep her head on straight!"

Carrie giggled. Her father had never let her forget the time she had overheard two women talking about a disorganized traveling salesman. She had spent weeks watching the salesman. Not once did she catch him when he didn't "have his head on straight," as the women had said.

The Talbots picked up their bags and made their way down the gangplank. Mr. Talbot led the way past bales of cotton and huge crates of furniture. At the edge of the dock, he helped both Carrie and her mother up onto the wooden boardwalk.

Carrie half walked, half skipped ahead of her father and mother. Her eyes darted everywhere, trying to see as much as possible. The sidewalk was almost as crowded as the rail of the *River Queen*. The stores were crowded with men, women, and children. The dirt streets were packed with prairie schooners, buckboards, and freight wagons.

"So many," Mrs. Talbot said in amazement. "I just didn't realize there would be so many people going West."

"It's the time of year," Mr. Talbot answered. "The spring thaw brought fresh green grass across the prairie. The grass will feed the oxen on the way. And it's safer to travel in large numbers. We'll find a wagon train and join it."

Mrs. Talbot touched her purse. "I have the list of things we need from the general store."

"You go ahead and locate some of the things, Martha. I'll head for the blacksmith to get a team and a wagon." He turned to Carrie. "You help your mother, Carrie."

"Yes, Pa," Carrie said. Mrs. Talbot stopped at a store. The sign painted on the window promised that all their traveling needs could be taken care of inside.

"Coming from the East?" Carrie read out loud. "Going to the West? Come on in. Give your feet a rest."

Carrie looked at her mother and they both laughed.

"Well, this ought to do," Martha Talbot said. "Come, Carrie. We've some serious shopping to do."

Carrie followed her mother into the store. After an hour or so she grew tired of paper and pins, pots and pans. She sat down on a barrel and swung her feet. Her eyes sparkled with interest as she watched the customers in the store.

After a few moments, she felt a tug at her foot. She looked down. A crawling baby pulled at her skirt. Carrie picked him up and held him in her lap. She laughed as he pulled at her bonnet strings. His gurgling reply brought a woman through the crowd.

"There you are, Joseph Edward," she said in an anxious voice. "I'm so sorry. I just can't keep my eyes on them all and hunt for what I need, too."

Mrs. Talbot turned. When she saw the baby in Carrie's lap, she smiled. "Carrie will take care of him while you make your purchases," she said. "Don't fret, now. She's very good with the little ones."

"Oh, thank you," the woman said in relief. "I won't be much longer."

She made her way back to the counter. Carrie tickled the baby's fat chin. His laugh was like running water. She played with him for a while. Before long, the baby began to squirm to get down. Carrie got up to walk him around the store.

A tall boy shoved his way through the crowd. He bumped into Carrie. He was about to push past her when he saw the baby. He frowned.

"Just what are you doing with Joseph Edward?" he demanded.

Carrie's eyebrows drew together in a frown as dark as the boy's. An angry reply flew to her tongue. Before the sharp words could come out, she took a deep breath. Her answer came in a perfect copy of her mother's quiet tone. "I'm taking care of him for the woman over there."

"He's *my* brother. *I'll* take him." The boy took the baby so quickly that Joseph Edward whimpered. Then the boy thrust his way through the people to the woman at the counter. He spoke so sharply that Carrie heard him clearly.

"Pa didn't buy the horse. He bought another team of oxen instead!"

His mother's reply was lost in a shout from outside. Carrie saw the boy hand the baby to his mother and stalk away. Two white-headed girls about Carrie's age hurried through the door. They went straight to the counter. One took the baby as the woman paid for her purchases.

The woman had not bought much. She gathered up the one small package. Holding on to the two girls beside her, she wended her way back to Carrie. The towheaded girls gave Carrie shy grins.

"Thank you, honey," the woman said breathlessly. "You're a right smart girl, to be as young as you are."

"Thank you," Carrie said. She stood up and held herself tall as her mother approached.

"Well, you surely did a fine job with Joseph Edward. I would never have finished without you," the woman said warmly. "I think this is the last of it. It'll have it be. We leave in a few days."

Mrs. Talbot stopped beside Carrie.

"I'm Martha Talbot, and this is my daughter, Carrie," she said. "We just came in on the boat."

"Glad to meet you. I'm Emma Gantz," the woman replied. "We came overland a week ago."

"Which train are you with?" Mrs. Talbot asked.

"The Thadler wagons," Mrs. Gantz replied. "It's a good train. Mr. Thadler hired an experienced wagon master. We expect a good crossing."

"Is it full? Could it handle one more?"

"Why, yes," Mrs. Gantz said. "A family turned back yesterday. The wife was sick. You might take their place."

"I'll tell my husband," Mrs. Talbot said. "If he hasn't found another place, perhaps we'll see you again."

The woman nodded and hurried out. Carrie watched the children following her and smiled. It would be fun to play with the children on the long trip. She wondered if the oldest girl was her age. Then her frown returned as she remembered the rude boy. He would not be fun at all!

Chapter Two
Dusty Trails

Carrie's mother finished her purchases. Carrie helped her carry the packages. They left the main street and walked toward the blacksmith shop. A shout from a passing wagon made them stop and stare.

"It's Pa!" Carrie said. "He got the wagon!"

Mr. Talbot stopped and waited for them to cross over to him. The oxen shuffled patiently as he helped his wife and daughter aboard. Carrie crawled through the canvas flap and tumbled down to the wooden floor. She squealed in delight.

"It's like a hideout," she said happily. "Just look at all this room!"

"Wait until all that room is full of supplies," her father said. "We don't have to worry about furniture, but we do have to take supplies to the mission. The wagon will be packed as tightly as all the rest by the time we leave."

He cracked the whip and the oxen began to plod along. "God was with us, Martha," he said to his wife. "I got the wagon and oxen at a good price and found a place on a wagon train. Seems like a family took sick and turned back. They sold out and are taking the steamer home. This is their outfit."

"Were they with the Thadler train?" Mrs. Talbot asked.

"Sure were," Mr. Talbot said, surprised. "How did you know?"

"We met a Mrs. Gantz from the wagon train. She told us the wagon master had made the crossing many times. It sounds good, Nathan," she replied.

"Then we're on our way." Mr. Talbot gave a gleeful shout. "O give thanks unto the Lord, for He is good, for His mercy endureth forever!"

Carrie popped her head out of the canvas opening. "What is it, Pa?" she asked.

"We're headed West, young lady," Mr. Talbot replied. "We're headed West."

The next two days were busy ones. Carrie had no time for visiting the other wagons. She helped pack bacon in barrels of bran. She helped pack eggs one by one in barrels of cornmeal. She helped fold and store blankets and ground sheets.

She helped boil butter and skim it until it was clear as oil. Then she poured the clear butter into cans. When the cans were sealed, she and her mother stacked them carefully in the wagon.

It took all of the two days to pack the wagon with hundred-pound sacks of flour, waterproofed bags of sugar, kegs of molasses, vinegar, spices, coffee, and other supplies needed at the mission.

When they finished, there was barely room to get about in the wagon. To save space, Mrs. Talbot sewed pockets and slings on the inside of the canvas. In them she stored the clothes they would be wearing on the trip.

One special pocket was made near the front. Mrs. Talbot sewed it carefully with double stitching. Then she wrapped the family Bible in oilcloth. She placed it in the snug pocket.

"What do you think, Carrie?" she said. "Won't the Bible be safe here? And right handy for reading, too."

The large family Bible had been entrusted to Carrie's care. Carrie took her responsibility seriously. Each morning, it was her job to bring the Bible to her father for the morning reading. And after the night reading, it was her job to put the Bible away carefully.

"It's your heritage," her father had told her. "In it are recorded the births and deaths of our people for a hundred years. On the day of your marriage it will be yours to keep."

So Carrie inspected the pocket carefully. When she was sure that the Bible would be safe, she nodded solemnly. With this final chore, everything was in order.

At four in the morning of the third day, Carrie woke to the sound of rifle fire. She sat up quickly and scrambled to the tailgate.

A lantern shed a circle of light on the ground near the wagon. Carrie could see her mother folding the quilts and ground cover. Her father strode away into the darkness.

"Ma! What was that?" Carrie whispered.

"The signal to wake up and get ready," her mother answered. "Your father has gone for the oxen. We'll soon be on our way."

Carrie peered into the darkness. Across the circle other lamps were lit. Shadowy forms moved back and forth in the pale light.

Quickly she dressed and hurried to help her mother. Smoke from the breakfast fires soon drifted skyward. The camp became a hubbub of activity. By seven, the camps were cleared and the wagons ready.

Carrie sat tensely on the wagon seat between her parents. A bugle sounded and the wagons began to roll, one by one. Riders raced ahead of the wagons. The wagons creaked on behind at a snail's pace. Shouts of triumph went up as the wagons finally lumbered onto the vast prairie land.

The slow pace jangled Carrie's nerves. It didn't take long for her to realize it was just as fast to walk as to ride—and a lot easier on the bones. When she saw others climb down to walk beside the wagons, she turned to her mother eagerly.

"There's Mrs. Gantz, Ma," Carrie said. "Let's catch up with her."

Two wagons up, they slowed to a walk beside the thin woman and her children. The two girls, Meg and Laura, gave Carrie welcoming smiles. The boy, Peter, hardly noticed her. He walked beside the oxen with his father. From time to time, he cracked a whip to keep the beasts moving. All the time he watched the riders racing back and forth.

"They'll wear those horses out before we stop for the nooning," he said.

"Don't fret, Peter," his father said, sighing. "You'll get your horse someday."

Carrie felt uncomfortable around Peter. "Let's go play," she said to the girls.

"Keep in sight, Carrie," Mrs. Talbot called. "We have enough adventure today without losing girls!"

"We will, Ma," Carrie answered.

Carrie ran into the billowy grass. Meg and Laura were right behind her. Over and over they rolled in its springy softness. When they tired of running, they came back for Joseph Edward.

The girls took turns carrying the baby. They ran up the line of wagons and sat in the grass to plait crowns of wildflowers. Joseph Edward crawled around them, scattering the petals in the wind. When their own wagons caught up, they would pick Joseph Edward up and run again.

When the wagon circled for the nooning, all three were hungry and worn out. Carrie was thankful to return to her own cook fire. After lunch, she curled up in the wagon to nap.

The first days were slow and easy. The ground was flat and the trail clear. A blue sky stretched over the flower-spangled earth. On Sunday the wagon master asked Carrie's father to hold a service. Mr. Talbot preached about

the majesty of God. Carrie had never felt closer to God than when she was standing under that great blue bowl of sky.

The rains began later in the week. It was as if the heavens opened and let loose all the water in the world. It fell in sheets, driving sideways in the wind. Lightning lit the sky in noonlike flashes. The horses were spooked and had to be held down. The canvas flapped back and forth in the gusts of wind.

Carrie loved it. She checked the pocket at the front of the wagon to make sure the Bible was safe from the rain. Then she huddled under the canvas in the back and watched the storm.

The trail turned into a shallow river. The oxen plodded on, the wagons churning through mud. At night Carrie held a ground sheet over the fire so her mother could cook.

Then the sun came out again. The trail dried and the grass was greener than ever. They reached Alcove Spring a few days later.

Carrie stood open-mouthed, looking at the waterfall. "I've never seen anything like it," she told the girls.

"Look, the boys are climbing the rocks," Laura said.

"Then so can we! Let's go!" Carrie said. She sat down and stripped off her shoes and stockings. With Laura and little Meg scrambling behind, she clawed her way up the side of the waterfall. They sat on a jutting rock and let the icy spray blow over them.

"Caroline Elizabeth!" Mrs. Talbot called from the bank. "What do you think you're doing? Get down from there!"

Reluctantly the girls clambered down, almost slipping on the wet rock. Carrie was last. She stopped to look back at the spring. "I'll always remember this place," she said to herself. "Always."

The wagon train moved on. It crossed the Big Blue River and followed the south bank of the Platte River. On either side the land stretched away to the sky. Herds of buffalo came close to the slow-moving wagons and then thundered away.

But nothing gave the children greater delight than the huge prairie-dog town. Even Peter was fascinated by the little animals. He took the girls out to the town. They walked in amazement among the hills of barking prairie dogs.

After they passed the prairie-dog town, life settled into a camp routine. Carrie had her chores. After she had done them, she played with her friends. Each night her mother taught her to read from the Bible. Each week her father taught her a new verse to hide in her heart.

Whenever the scout for the wagon train was in camp, he taught the children the sign language of the Plains Indians. Carrie's father was pleased. He practiced with her until he could make the motions as quickly as she could. When the scout understood the reason for their interest, he traded lessons in the Cheyenne language for a place at Martha's cook fire.

"Keep your eyes and ears open," Mr. Talbot told Carrie. "We need to learn as much as we can before we reach the mission. You never know what the Lord can use later. And this can be a harsh country if you walk through it blind to what is going on around you."

The weeks went by. They passed Chimney Rock in late June. The wagons entered Fort Laramie two days later. Beyond the fort, the trail led into the Rockies. The wagons jolted along over rocks and dry sand. Wagon wheels broke. Wagon tongues sheared off. Oxen strained to pull their heavy loads.

"Lighten the load!" became the daily cry.

Everyone walked to spare the oxen. Yet even that was not enough. Carrie stared as families gently set cherished furniture beside the trail. Some women went on with hard, set faces; others cried.

Mr. Talbot stopped beside Carrie as she wiped the dust from a discarded clock.

"Look, Pa," she said. "It has pretty flowers on the face. And it chimes. Listen."

She wound the clock. Silvery music tinkled in the air. "How could anyone bear to give this up?"

"These things are of this world only, Carrie," her father told her gently. "Set your heart on things above, never on worldly treasure. For where your treasure is, there your heart will be also."

Carrie carefully set the clock on a discarded oak dresser. They went on up the trail. Carrie listened for the chimes as long as she could. But all too soon, she could hear only the sound of the wagon wheels on the rocks.

Chapter Three

Warrior's Moon

At Sweetwater River, the travel became easier. The wagons turned along the flatland and followed the river. The last week in June the wagon train reached the town of Independence Rock. The wagons circled on the plain outside the fort. Meg and Laura followed as Carrie crawled up the rock. They scribbled their names beside those of earlier travelers.

"You have to put the date too," Laura said. "Everyone else did."

Carrie nodded. She pushed her hair out of her eyes and scratched, *June 30, 1853.*

That night Carrie counted the days on her fingers. "What day is the Fourth of July?" she asked.

"Monday," her father replied. "There'll be a real celebration here."

"Can we stay?" Carrie asked eagerly.

Mr. Talbot shook his head. "The wagon master says we're running behind schedule as it is. Most folks'll celebrate tonight. How about it?"

"Well, I have some yeast put by," Mrs. Talbot said. "The sage hen and rabbit you brought in this morning would make a savory pie. And maybe we could have a pound cake. Our eggs are long gone, but I heard they have fresh eggs at the fort. They'll come dear, though."

"Special days are dear as well," Mr. Talbot said. "Get your eggs. We'll celebrate!"

Carrie jumped up and down. "Can we have guests? Like we did back home?"

"Why not?" Mr. Talbot laughed. "Ask the Gantz family, and the Greenes. I think they are short on supplies right now. And the Cantrells. Their baby could use some fresh milk."

By nightfall the spirit of celebration had spread through the entire camp. The gathering of families grew until all the wagon train joined the festivities. The children played games on the grassy meadows. The women brought out their best and baked as if they were home. They spread the ground sheets together to make a long table. Everyone shared what he had.

Carrie feasted on buffalo steak, savory pie, dried apple fritters, fried rabbit, and roasted sage hens. When she could hold no more, she curled up on a blanket to rest.

Meg and Laura came to sit with her. They lay back and watched a full moon drift in a velvety sky.

"It's a copper penny," Meg said.

"It's a silver medallion," Laura said.

"It's a savory pie," Carrie groaned, holding her stomach.

"Huh," Peter said sharply. He stepped out of the shadows near the wagon. "It's a warrior's moon."

Carrie rolled over to look at him. "How do you know that?"

"A trapper at the fort told me. He said the Indians use the moon to travel at night. They go long distances to raid the tipis of their enemies."

He reached down to jerk on one of Carrie's braids. "So watch your hair, Red," he said.

Carrie snatched her braid back and sat up. She stared at him as he walked away, laughing.

"Don't mind him," Laura said quietly. "Mom says he is growing too fast. It addles his mind."

"If you say so," Carrie said doubtfully. She lay back down to look up at the moon. This time it didn't look so round and yellow and friendly.

She went to bed that night with an aching head. The next morning she groaned when she heard the warning rifle shots. For a moment she thought about staying in bed. Outside she heard her mother starting the cook fire. Slowly she crawled out from under the blankets. Her mother took one look at her and sent her back to bed.

By the time the wagons were moving, she was burning with fever. For days she drifted in and out of sleep. When she awakened, a spoon was set gently against her teeth. She twisted, but the liquid still poured down her throat. Again she slept.

Finally the fever passed.

"You had cholera," Carrie's mother told her. "Praise God it was a light case."

Before a week had passed Carrie was eager to get out of the confining wagon. She set out in search of Laura and Meg. Neither of the girls was to be seen. Carrie found their wagon way up the line.

Mr. Gantz walked beside the oxen. His face was lined with worry. "Have you seen Peter?" he asked.

Carrie shook her head. "What's wrong?"

"Joseph Edward has a fever. I think it's cholera." He swallowed hard. "I sent Peter for the doctor."

Laura opened the flap of the wagon. Her face was frightened. "He's real bad, Pa," she said. "Ma wants to know if the doc is coming."

Mr. Gantz shaded his eyes. A rider came down the line of wagons. "He's here," he called to his wife. "He's coming!"

Carrie walked beside the wagon with Laura until the doctor came out. Laura told her that cholera had swept the wagon train in the last few weeks.

"Micah Evans died," Laura said. "And Toby Whitall. And little Anabelle Catlin."

She looked fearfully toward the wagon. The doctor climbed out and jumped to the ground.

"I left some medicine," he told Mr. Gantz, "but your wife is ill also. She must have help."

"I'll tell Ma," Carrie said. She ran back to the wagon. "Mrs. Gantz and Joseph Edward are sick," she told her mother. "They need nursing."

The wagon master heard her. He stopped beside the Talbot's wagon. "The Gantz wagon needs to be separated from the rest," he said. "And I need help up front. We've lost another man."

Mr. Talbot hesitated. "My wife will nurse the Gantz family. And I can go with you if Peter will drive my wagon."

The change was made. The Gantz wagon fell in behind the others. Laura and Meg rode with

Carrie in the Talbots' wagon. Peter drove it in line behind his family.

The girls played quietly as the wagon jolted along. By midmorning they tired of their games and lay side by side on the sacks of flour. Carrie watched a cloud of dust on the trail behind them.

"What's that behind us?" Carrie called to Peter. "Another wagon train?"

Peter jumped down to look. "It's the remuda. The horses," he said impatiently.

Carrie blinked and felt foolish. She knew as well as anyone that the extra horses were driven behind and allowed to graze during the day. At night they joined the oxen in the circle. She had just never ridden this far behind.

"Why are you stopping?" she asked Peter.

He gave her a defiant stare. "There's a roan horse that I want to see." He felt in his pocket for a lump of sugar.

The horses swept around an outcropping of rocks a hundred yards behind them. The men driving the horses fired shots into the air. Only then did the children see the danger. Painted riders appeared at the crest of the hill.

"Indians!" Peter yelled, and he leaped onto the wagon seat. But they had lingered behind too long. The wagon train had rolled on across the ridge. Peter grabbed the whip from its socket and lashed it across the backs of the oxen. They fell into a trot.

The girls were slung back and forth in the wagon. Meg began to cry. Carrie tried to steady herself long enough to reach across to the younger girl. She pushed her down between the barrel of meal and bags of seed.

"Hang on," Carrie shouted as Laura slid across the sacks of flour. Behind them they heard shrill yelps and shrieks. A gunshot ricocheted off a rock.

Peter cracked the whip. The wagon jolted over the rocky trail. Carrie caught a glimpse of the horses. They were coming fast, hemmed in on both sides by the remuda drivers.

She turned and peered out the flap. The wagon swayed over the ridge. Below them they saw the wagon train on flat ground. It had begun circling for protection.

Their wagon picked up speed going downhill. It tilted and grazed a huge boulder. The canvas on the right side tore with a sickening sound.

Carrie whirled to see the canvas flopping loose. The pocket that held the Bible was dangling over the side of the wagon.

Carrie lunged across the wagon. She caught hold of one of the bare ribs of the top and reached for the pocket. On the first try she missed. The wagon swayed again, and she fell forward. Her hand closed on the Bible.

The wagon jolted over another outcropping of rock. Carrie slipped and fell, still clutching the dangling pocket. The canvas ripped, and Carrie swung out over the side. Then the canvas gave way completely and she was dumped onto bare ground.

Carrie cradled the Bible in her arms. She rolled into the shelter of the rocks. The remuda horses and their riders plunged over the ridge behind her. They thundered past and disappeared down the trail.

Shakily Carrie got to her knees and tried to stand up. Dust clogged her nose, and her loosened hair filled her mouth. But before she could run for better cover, the party of Indians charged down the slope.

One of them almost ran her down. She thrust the Bible up to protect her head. The Indian's horse stumbled and fell. Its short, muscular rider sprawled in the dust. The fallen Indian scrambled up with a yell of rage. He rushed at Carrie, eyes glittering. Carrie tried to run, but fear glued her feet to the rocky ground. She closed her eyes as the Indian raised his knife.

The blow never came. Another rider had shouldered his horse between Carrie and her attacker. The man with the knife snarled and glared up at the rider. But the tall lean Indian on the horse faced Carrie's attacker without a sign of fear.

Carrie felt the rider's strong arm sweep across her back. A moment later she found herself seated in front of the tall Indian. There was no escape. Her unbound hair whipped back as the horse lunged after the others. Still clutching her Bible, Carrie rode off in the midst of the raiders.

Chapter Four

Lodgepoles by the River

The ground spun by under the galloping hooves. Each hill, each river, each outcropping of rock seemed to rush up, then disappear. Even when the Indians slowed their pace, the rest that Carrie expected never came.

They rode straight through the night. At first light, the Indians stopped. They turned the horses loose to graze. Carrie staggered and fell when the tall Indian took her off the horse. He picked her up and carried her to the shade of a cottonwood tree. He brought water from the shallow stream. Carrie drank eagerly.

One of the other Indians said something that Carrie could not understand. The young warrior turned to face them. They fell silent.

He sat down next to Carrie and reached for the Bible. Carrie's fingers tightened and she jerked back. The Indian stood up. "Strong medicine," he said. "Made war horse stumble."

Then he pointed to himself and the man that had attacked Carrie. He drew his finger across his arm. Carrie recognized the scout's sign language for "Cheyenne." He pointed to the remaining three Indians and drew his finger across his throat. "Sioux," he said.

Carrie had fallen into the hands of a raiding party. The two young Cheyenne were on their first raid, in the company of Sioux friends. They had hoped to bring back horses to impress their tribe.

Their only prize was Carrie. Her captor touched her hair. Carrie had endured enough jokes from Peter to know that her hair would be admired by the Indians. She felt the blood drain out of her face. Her head spun with both hunger and fear. She clutched the Bible and shrank back from the young Indian. The Indian let the strand of hair go and walked back to the others.

Carrie sat huddled weakly where he had left her. They had come miles across land that was a wilderness to her. She didn't know where to go even if she could run. She rested her head on the Bible.

"Pa," she whispered, "Come and get me."

I will call upon the Lord, who is worthy to be praised: so shall I be saved from mine enemies.

The words sounded clearly in her mind. Carrie jerked her head up, expecting to see her father. There was no one in sight except the Cheyenne and Sioux warriors.

Carrie closed her eyes and thought about her father. She remembered how often he had repeated this verse before he prayed out loud. She ran her fingers over the Bible. Ashamed, she realized that she had not once prayed. She closed her eyes.

In the middle of her prayer, she felt a rough hand on her arm. Before she could resist, she was once again lifted onto the Indian's horse. In one spring, the Indian was behind her.

They galloped across the sandbar onto the other bank. Carrie twisted to look behind her. There was no sign of pursuit as far as she could see. She turned back.

Two long days later, they reached another creek. This one ran from the mountains, bubbling and twisting over rocky ground. At a fork in the creek, the Indians parted. The three Sioux turned south. The two Cheyenne headed into the foothills with Carrie.

They came to a broad valley. The creek snaked through the middle of the valley. They had reached the edge of a village. Carrie could see that tipis edged the creek banks on both sides. Smoke rose in lazy plumes from the cook fires outside the tipis.

For a moment, everything seemed peaceful. But then the two warriors began a shrill song and kicked their horses into a run. Frightened, Carrie clung to her captor. The two warriors raced their horses through the village and back, and their yells vibrated in the still air.

Finally they stopped in the center of the village and dismounted. Carrie's captor lifted her high into the air for all to see.

"I, Swift Arrow, have brought you the daughter of the sun," he called. "Come and see!"

The Cheyenne people murmured and pointed at Carrie's hair. The other warrior scowled. She heard someone call his name—it was Lone Wolf. Carrie met his eyes. They glared back at her, black as burnt coals. As Carrie's feet touched the ground, he darted forward.

Carrie screamed. She tried desperately to break away from the young Indian without losing her grip on the Bible. He shook her roughly. Outcries arose from the crowd. Then some of the onlookers grabbed the man and held him.

Angrily Lone Wolf shook off the restraining hands. He snatched for the reins of his horse and stalked away. He yelled something back at the villagers, but they only laughed. They turned back to Carrie's captor.

"I have brought you the daughter of the sun," Swift Arrow told the chief. "She holds a medicine bundle of amazing power."

The chief studied both man and girl for a moment. The noise around them faded to a respectful silence. Finally he raised his hand. An old man stepped out of the crowd.

"You were the keeper of the arrows that were stolen from our tribe," the chief said to the old man. "From that day the buffalo child has given us only a portion of what we once had. The deer fly before our hunting arrows. Our warriors return empty-handed. Now your grandson has brought a strange gift to our village. What do you say, Keeper? Will this medicine replace that which we lost?"

The old man put his hand on Carrie's shoulder. She looked at his face. His eyes were kind. When he held out his hand for the Bible, she did not resist. He turned it over and over in his hands. Then he carefully unwrapped the oilskin and lifted the cover.

The Cheyenne waited in silence as he paged through the book. Carrie held her breath as he stopped to inspect one of the fancy letters that began each chapter. At last he handed the Bible back to Carrie.

The old man faced the chief and spoke with authority. "Many moons ago, I saw a book such as this. It belonged to a teacher of the heart at Fort Laramie. It contains the words of the Great Spirit."

"Then it is indeed strong medicine," the chief said. "Take the child and her medicine bundle to your lodge. They will remain there with you until I decide what must be done."

Carrie had not understood all of the words, although she recognized some that the scout had taught them. But she saw the reverence with which the Bible was treated. Her spirits lifted.

The Cheyenne moved back to allow her to follow the old man. He led her to a lodge near the center of the village. It was large and well-constructed, as befitting a man of power in the tribe.

"Come," he said to Carrie. She followed him inside. At one side of the tipi, skins had been piled for beds. Carrie sat down limply. The old man stepped outside and called a name.

A woman appeared. Her dark eyes inspected Carrie shyly. On her back, a baby slept in a light cradle. In her hands she held a platter of smoked meat. She handed it to Carrie carefully.

The smell of the meat knotted Carrie's stomach. She had eaten only dried meat and raw berries on the trail. She reached for the plate greedily.

As she ate, two small children peered around the flap of the tipi. The woman looked up and saw them. Her quiet words sent the children scurrying away.

The old man motioned to the bed. "You sleep," he said. Carrie guessed at what he meant and nodded. The old man went out of the tipi. The woman followed and Carrie was alone.

She lay down on the skins. As tired as she was, her mind raced to and fro. Where were her rescuers? What would happen to her? Why was she being treated so well?

She lay alone for what seemed like hours. She was afraid to close her eyes. When she finally did, the faces of the Indians swam across her closed eyelids. She saw the old man, the two warriors, the chief, a child in the crowd, the baby on the woman's back.

The Indian baby had reminded her of Joseph Edward. The memory of cholera seemed so far away. She wondered if the baby was still alive. Numbly she began to pray for him and for the others on the wagon train. Peace came with the prayers, and she slept.

She awoke to shadows. When her eyes adjusted to the dimness, she saw the old man sitting near her. He was holding the Bible. Carrie sat up in alarm. He looked up and smiled at her to show that he meant no harm. She lay back, her bones aching.

She watched as the woman entered and went about her work quietly. The children that had peered around the flap earlier slipped inside the tipi. They stayed as far away from her as they could. In surprise, she realized that they were afraid of her.

The old man called the children to him. "You must not fear a guest in our lodge," he told them. They regarded him wide-eyed.

Carrie saw them look from the old man to her. In response to his urging, they moved forward. "Laughing Water," the old man said. "Small Bird."

First one spoke; then the other. Carrie smiled cautiously, knowing that the words were words of welcome. "Thank you," she said, trying out the words she had practiced with the scout.

The woman nodded in approval, and the children hurried to her side. They settled on the floor beside her. She gave them some painted sticks. They began to play. The woman went back to the baby.

The old man pointed to the woman. "Sky Woman. Little One."

Carrie said the syllables after him. She remembered how her father had urged her to listen and learn and was glad for the few words of Cheyenne that she already knew. She watched the Indian family carefully.

Only when Swift Arrow entered did she stiffen again. She gazed at him warily. When he settled down without bothering her, she lay back again. After a while, she decided he was the woman's eldest son. She wondered where the father was and what he would be like. She watched the entrance to the tipi nervously. The evening drifted into a long, lonely night. No one else came.

Chapter Five

The Medicine Bundle

Carrie woke early. The camp was still. She stared up into darkness and thought about her parents. It would be rising time for the wagon train. She closed her eyes and imagined the glow of light from the wagon lantern. Her mother's face smiled at her. From the other side of the wagon came the sound of her father's voice as he sang quietly.

"They're with me," she thought. "If I can just keep remembering."

She rolled over and stared into the darkness, her throat aching with unshed tears. "I'll listen," she said fiercely. "I'll learn. And I'll find out how to get to the mission by myself."

Something moved. She lay still as it squirmed closer to her. It was the smallest girl. Murmuring in her sleep, she was seeking the warmth of another body. She felt like Joseph Edward did when he wanted to cuddle. Carrie drew her close and lay back down.

When dawn brightened the tipi, the child woke and looked up at Carrie. The brown eyes opened wide. Carrie touched the little brown nose and smiled.

Across the tipi the others were moving. Carrie got up stiffly. "Good morning," she said firmly. Her greeting was returned in Cheyenne. She listened carefully. She repeated the syllables.

The old man looked pleased. His keen eyes fixed on her. They were as dark as the eyes of the warrior that had attacked Carrie. But they gleamed with the warmth of a summer night. Carrie smiled at him, her fear gone.

The young man took his bow and arrows and left the lodge. The old man watched him go. "Swift Arrow," he said to Carrie. His hands moved in sign language. Carrie was even more certain that the warrior was Sky Woman's son.

Sky Woman sent the children to gather brush for the fire. Carrie went with them. No one tried to stop her or to restrain her in any way. Carrie's heart beat faster as they approached the edge of camp.

She looked wistfully at the shadowy trees. Then she sighed. Common sense told her that she would be recaptured in a matter of minutes. And that she would never be able to find her way back to the Oregon Trail alone.

Outside the camp the girls picked up deadwood from the ground. Carrie pointed to the wood. Laughing Water told her the Indian word. Carrie said it over and over.

At first Laughing Water looked puzzled. Then, as Carrie kept trying, the syllables sounded more like the Cheyenne word for firewood. Laughing Water laughed. Carrie smiled. She was glad Laughing Water thought it was a game. It would make it easier to learn.

All day Carrie worked and played with the children. She repeated everything they said out loud until she got the rhythm of the words right. Then she said them only to herself.

An extra pair of hands in the tipi freed Sky Woman from some of her chores. When she finished, she sat down outside the tipi with buckskin and an awl. Carrie came to watch her work.

The woman's thin hands flew in and out as she bound the edges of the buckskin. She worked a design of beads and feathers into one side of the buckskin. Then she put fringe along the other edge. Long thongs completed the design.

She motioned to Carrie. Carrie followed her inside. The woman handed Carrie the decorated buckskin and pointed to the Bible. When Carrie handed the Bible to her, Sky Woman wrapped the Bible in the buckskin. Then she hung it to the lodgepole over the skins where Carrie had slept.

"Thank you," Carrie said. She touched the beadwork admiringly.

Sky Woman gave her a happy smile. She touched Carrie's clothes. Then she touched hers.

"I will make you strong clothes," she said. "Cheyenne clothes."

Carrie understood her meaning, even though Sky Woman had spoken so swiftly that she had not caught all the words. After the woman left the tipi, Carrie looked at the deerskin cover uneasily. She realized that the buckskin kept the Bible up out of harm's way. Still, it looked too much like the medicine bundle that hung from the center pole. She shivered.

"It's the Bible," she said out loud. "Not a medicine bundle. Not some Indian superstition."

She took it out and held it. Memories of the daily readings overwhelmed her. "I'll read it myself," she determined. "Every day. Just like Ma and Pa. Out loud."

Carrie found a quiet place on the bank of the creek. She lay down in the thick grass. She found the marker her father had left. She began to read. At first some of the names sounded strange and unwieldy as she tried to sound them out. Then memory prompted her reading, and the long known phrases began to roll off her tongue.

She did not hear the old man approach. Only when he sat beside her did she look up.

"Go on," he motioned.

Carrie began to read again. At first she was nervous. But the old man sat without moving. After a time, she forgot he was there. She stopped when her throat grew tired.

It was dusk and an early night breeze ruffled the grass. Carrie realized that she had been reading at the same time her parents usually read to her. She put her head down on her arms and cried.

When Carrie looked up, the old man was gone. She dried her tears quickly. It was near dark. She picked up the Bible and started toward the camp.

From the corner of her eye she saw the shadow of a young man. He moved from behind a nearby tree trunk. She tried to get a glimpse of him without turning around, but she could not. She sensed him following as she hurried back to the safety of the campfires. As he disappeared into the throng of lodges, she caught sight of him. It was Swift Arrow.

The little girls ran up to meet her. They stopped shyly as she approached. Carrie scooped Small Bird up. The child clung to one arm and wrapped her thin legs around Carrie's waist. Carrie went inside the tipi and tucked her Bible into the buckskin cover. Then she carried the child back to the campfire.

Other days passed much the same. Carrie played with the children and helped around the camp. The young man came and went. Carrie spoke to him only when he spoke to her.

She learned more of the language. And she learned everything she could about the camp. She noticed that the cook pot at their tipi was always full. Many others in the village were not.

"My son is a good provider. He has good medicine," Sky Woman said. "Soon he will have no need to ride north with Lone Wolf and the others. Soon he will be a chief."

Carrie had seen the other warrior around the camp. Although he glared at her, he kept out of her way. She pulled her face down into a fierce scowl. "Lone Wolf?" she asked.

Sky Woman laughed. "Lone Wolf," she agreed. "Bad man."

When Sky Woman finished the leggings and fringed dress, Carrie put them on. Beaded moccasins completed her costume. Now she ran as freely as Laughing Water. The sun darkened her pale skin, but nothing could tame her flaming hair. Sky Woman could pick her out in a crowd of running children with no trouble at all.

At chokecherry picking time, the tribe moved to the Black Hills. Carrie helped pick the berries with the other children. Little One was no longer in his cradle board on his mother's back. Now he clung to Carrie as firmly as his sister, Small Bird, did. Carrie fed him ripe chokecherries and laughed when the juice ran down his chin.

The afternoon sun beat down on the hillside. The women pounded the chokecherries into pulp. They spread the pulp on flat rocks to dry in the sun.

Carrie took the smallest children to the shade. They rolled on thick beds of pine needles. She now knew enough of their language to tell them simple stories. She told them of Peter and

Moses and Jesus. They listened and begged for more.

She was telling them about the miracle of the two fish and five loaves. Little One grew restless and squirmed in her lap. She let him down and went on with her story. Before she finished, a wail startled her. She looked up to see Sky Woman running down the hill toward them.

Carrie whirled around. Little One had crawled out of the sheltering shade. He had pulled up on one of the rock slabs. His face was smeared with juice, and he was scooping up tiny handfuls of chokecherry pulp. He looked back at Carrie happily.

Then Carrie saw why Sky Woman was running. A brown bear had lumbered out of the woods. Attracted by the cherries, he headed straight for the drying pulp. And Little One was in his way.

Carrie saw that the bear would reach the cherries before Sky Woman. Frantically she looked around. At her feet were fallen branches. She picked up the largest one she could carry.

Yelling as loudly as she could, she ran toward Little One. Little One's eyes went round, and he burst into tears. Behind him, the bear stopped. It watched Carrie, nose upraised.

The other children had followed Carrie. Branches in hand, the children ran toward the bear. It gave up and shuffled off toward the sheltering shade.

That night Swift Arrow sat at their campfire. He listened to the Keeper's tale of Carrie's courage. He watched Little One playing at Sky Woman's feet.

He got up and took one of the eagle feathers from his coup stick. He said something to Sky Woman. She smiled in approval. A few quick movements of her hand attached the feather to thongs and a beaded circle. She called Carrie to her.

"My oldest son gives this to you," she said, "to tell the tribe of your courage in saving his brother. He says your medicine is stronger than he thought."

Carrie stood still as Sky Woman attached the feather to her braid. "Thank you," she said quietly.

Swift Arrow nodded. He left the lodge. Carrie watched him go. She wondered what he meant by strong medicine. Her eyes sought the Bible swinging from its buckskin cradle. Then she looked at the Cheyenne medicine bundle that hung from the center lodgepole.

"If medicine means spiritual help," she said to herself, "then he is right. For my help comes from the one and only true God. And He is with me. I know it."

Chapter Six

Daughter of the Sun

In the dying days of summer, the old man fell sick. He burned with fever until his skin seemed paper thin. The trips to the sweat lodges to kill the fever only weakened him.

Sky Woman was afraid. "He will die," she told Swift Arrow. "He is not strong enough to make the trip back to the river."

Swift Arrow hung his bow on a lodgepole and knelt beside his grandfather. The eyes that stared back at him were glassy. The old man tried to move but fell back weakly.

Little One began to cry. "Sh," Carrie said. She shifted him on her hip. "Out," she said to the two little girls. "We play."

She let them lead the way through the camp. Above them the tops of the dark craggy mountains were veiled in the mist of early morning. The days were shorter now, and the grass on the hills was brown. It was time for the tribe to seek the warmer flatlands to the south.

When Small Bird stopped to chase a friend, Carrie saw dried chokecherries and pemmican packed in neat reed baskets beside the flap of the tipi. She saw that the stretched hides of slain deer and beaver had been taken down and packed in bales.

Laughing Water saw them too. She came to hold Carrie's hand. Carrie saw the frightened look in the brown eyes, but she had no answer for what troubled the child. She had prayed often for the old man's recovery, but he was still sick. There was nothing she could do.

"Come," she called to Small Bird. Reluctantly, Small Bird left her playmate and followed them through the camp.

Lone Wolf's tipi was close to the edge of the camp. He sat outside, sharpening a knife. He watched them approach. Even the fearless Small Bird scurried back to Carrie as the young man made a face at her.

Carrie's head went up, and her back stiffened. The savage young man knew she was afraid of him. She had no intention of letting him know how much he scared her. As they passed, he made a sudden motion toward her with the knife. Laughing Water and Small Bird shrank back against Carrie. Little One began to cry. Carrie kept on walking. One step at a time, she said to herself.

Lone Wolf laughed as she hurried in spite of all her efforts. "Daughter of the sun!" he called mockingly. "Your hair will brighten my lodgepole some winter night!"

The girls broke into a run. Outside the camp they shook off their fear of the warrior and climbed the rocks. It was leaf-falling time. The aspens and maples in the hills blazed with red and yellow.

The girls gathered red and brown and orange and yellow leaves. Laughing Water strung them into brightly colored headbands. Small Bird stuffed them inside Little One's shirt and leggings. The girls laughed when he waddled back and forth, looking like a fat brown bear. Little One broke into gurgling chuckles as the leaves tickled him.

When they returned to the camp, the people had gathered in front of the chief's lodge. "It is leaf-falling time," he told them. "Soon the pale moon will ride the night wind. The buffalo will graze southward to the land of the Comanche. Snow will come from the mountains. We must return to the valley. There we will be sheltered from the winter storms."

"Will the Keeper be able to make the journey south?" Lone Wolf asked. His voice was smooth and quiet. Carrie did not understand why it scared her more than when he was angry.

Swift Arrow spoke from behind Carrie. "The Keeper will remain here with us. We will join you when he is able to travel."

"The Crows raid southward during leaf-falling time." Lone Wolf's voice was as slick as bear grease. "You will not be safe alone."

Swift Arrow frowned. "I will remain here. I will take care of my family."

Lone Wolf stepped back with a satisfied smile on his face. "As you wish, brother."

The chief nodded. "As you wish," he said kindly. "We will await your return to our lodges."

After the others were gone, the nights were quiet. Inside the tipi, Carrie told her stories over and over again. And she read aloud.

The Keeper liked the rhythm of the language. Carrie watched him and found herself wishing that he could understand the words that he heard. She remembered her father's dream of translating the Bible into the Indian languages.

Carrie decided to translate Psalm 91 into Cheyenne. She spent hours struggling with her words. Her progress was slow and stumbling. She pestered Sky Woman and the girls for words. They began to find other work to do when they saw her coming with the Bible in her hand.

Carrie did not give up. Some words were easy, others were difficult, and some simply could not be translated. But finally she felt that she had at least captured the meaning of the psalm.

When Carrie recited it in Cheyenne, the old man closed his eyes to listen. Wisps of smoke drifted in the tipi as the night wind nipped at the flap. Carrie coughed but the old man didn't move. He was lost in dreams of his youth.

"He was a great warrior," Sky Woman said quietly. "When our people were starving, he found the great herds of buffalo. He brought us here to this valley where our children have grown strong."

"But why isn't he chief?" Carrie whispered.

"He was. He could be now. But he chose to be Keeper of the Medicine Arrows. When the medicine bundle was stolen from our tribe, he fasted and prayed to the Great Spirit every day. He almost died."

"But he is still called the Keeper," Carrie said.

"Some of the arrows were returned, but not all."

Sky Woman's face was sad. "He felt that the Great Spirit no longer looked with favor on him. But now, you have come."

Carrie followed Sky Woman's gaze to the hanging Bible. "You have brought honor to his old age and peace to his heart."

"Only God can do that," Carrie said. "Not me."

Sky Woman looked puzzled. "But are not your God and the Great Spirit the same?"

On this subject Carrie was certain. Her father had often talked about the Great Spirit of the Indians. She shook her head. "No. There is only one God, who made all things."

"But the Great Spirit is the creator of all things." Sky Woman put her basket down. "He made the Earth Woman, the Buffalo Child, and even you, Daughter of the Sun."

Carrie searched her memory for the right words. "Most people believe there is a creator. But they do not know him. Instead they worship all sorts of things. They worship strange spirits, carved rocks, a certain animal or tree." She hesitated and then added, "Or even the sun. But those are not gods. God is real."

Sky Woman shrugged. "I know little of these things. Our women are not allowed to even gaze upon our medicine bundles when they are open. There is much I do not know. We will ask the Keeper."

Carrie looked across at the old man. His gray hair shadowed his face as his chin sank down on his chest. Little One scrambled onto his lap and woke the old man from his daydream. He shook his head slightly and picked up the child. Then he looked across the fire at Carrie as if he had never drifted off into his own world.

And Carrie finished the psalm as if she had never stopped. This time she tried to say the verses with the excitement her father had always used when he read or told stories. The old man listened, tired eyes shining, when she spoke about protection from arrows that fly by day. He clenched his fist in triumph when she spoke of the pestilence that walks by night.

"I will get well," he said fiercely. "I will get well."

Swift Arrow left the camp only to hunt. He brought back rabbits and sage hens to fill the cooking pot. The old man ate and steadily grew stronger. Soon he was sitting up. Once again he took a keen interest in what was going on around him.

After a few days, he called Carrie to his side.

"Sit with me," he said, "and talk."

Carrie sat down, her red braids gleaming in the firelight. Sky Woman had told him what Carrie had said about the Great Spirit. He had many questions for her. She remembered some of the answers from the lessons her father taught. To answer others, she searched the Bible for verses. Haltingly, she translated them.

As she spent more and more time reading the Bible, her thoughts turned to her parents. Never once did she think that they had gone back to the East. Someday she would find them at the mission. She was as certain of that as she was of her own name. She said it out loud over and over, rolling the sounds off her tongue: "Caroline Elizabeth Talbot. Caroline Elizabeth Talbot. Caroline Elizabeth Talbot."

Her thoughts brought back memories of the trip westward. She remembered the beautifully carved dressers that had been dumped by the trail when it became necessary to lighten the load. She remembered the clock she had picked up. She remembered how quickly the sound of the chimes had faded.

And she remembered the packing her mother had done for the trip West. Only a few clothes had been chosen. The rest of them and the household goods had been given to the needy. Even when her prized possessions left the house, her mother's face had reflected only peace. The words her mother had said to a questioning friend whispered on the wind outside the tipi.

. . . and be content with such things as ye have: for he hath said, I will never leave thee, nor forsake thee.

Carrie looked around at the simple tipi, at the few necessary possessions that could be easily packed and moved. She placed the Bible carefully in its sling. It was all she had. It was all she needed.

Chapter Seven
Wolves of Hunger

Carrie awoke to quiet. It pressed at her from all sides, like a live thing. She stared out at the strange light that filled the tipi. Something prickled against her eyelids, then her cheek. She sat up.

It was cold. Everyone else lay bundled up in thick layers of fur. Nothing moved in the tipi. Carrie started to lie back down when a spattering of prickles teased their way across her nose. She glanced up and saw flakes of white drifting down from the opening at the top of the tipi.

She threw back the furs and tiptoed to the flap. She pulled the flap back and looked out into a white world. Snow covered the bare trees in a blanket softer than the white fox skin Swift Arrow had brought home last week. It mounded over the rocks and drifted in banks next to the tree trunks.

A gust of wind dashed a flurry of flakes against her face, and she backed away. She bumped against something solid. She looked up and saw Swift Arrow. He reached out and held the flap for her.

"It's snowing," she said awkwardly.

"Yes. The snow came early this year." He smiled down at her. He pointed toward the sloping fields where they had picked choke-cherries warmed by the sun.

"Good sliding place."

Carrie looked startled. She glanced from him to the fields. "Sliding? Sledding?"

"We peel bark from the trees. Roll into sleds," he said. His eyes sparkled with memories. He chuckled. "I made a fine sled one year. I rubbed it with bear grease. My sled beat Lone Wolf's to the bottom every time."

Carrie laughed uncertainly. "I guess he didn't like that."

Swift Arrow agreed. "Lone Wolf does not like to be beaten. He wants to be chief some day. A chief must not be bested by anyone."

"But I thought you would be chief," Carrie said, "not Lone Wolf."

"He has brought back many horses, many coups. He is a good warrior."

"He won't be a good leader," Carrie said stubbornly. "He cares for no one but himself."

"The council will choose between us," Swift Arrow replied. "It will be their choice, not ours."

Behind them the fur beds began to tremble. Little One tumbled out first. Sleepy-eyed, he stumbled to lean against Swift Arrow's leg. Both hands clasped around the young man's knee.

"It's snowing," Carrie said. "It's snowing, Little One."

The little boy didn't answer. Swift Arrow looked down and grinned. "He went back to sleep," he said. He lifted the child and put him back down beside his mother.

Instantly awake, Small Bird and Laughing Water tumbled over each other to get to the door. Their shrieks of joy woke the others. The quiet burst like a pin-pricked bubble as they charged out into the drifts of snow.

Swift Arrow stripped the bark from a tree. He made sleds for each of them, rubbing them well with bear grease. The girls slid, laughing and shouting, down the hill.

When Little One cried, Swift Arrow made him a sled. He lifted the child onto it and sat behind him. Carrie stopped and stared as the young man and child slid down the hill and tumbled off into the snow. Little One clambered back on the sled. "Again," he said.

"Ride me," Small Bird demanded. "Your sled is faster."

"This sled is not faster," Swift Arrow said. "You put all weight on front of sled. Sled does not want to go. Look."

He shifted his weight. The sled moved. He leaned back. It stopped. "Now use weight to change directions."

The girls were soon careening down the hill with the confidence of snowshoe rabbits. Swift Arrow picked up Little One. He brushed snow and ice out of the child's thick, black hair and carried him back inside the tipi.

It snowed again that night and the next. Snow piled in drifts around the outside of the tipi. Swift Arrow met the Keeper's worried look. The snow had come too soon and too deep. Many animals would die from lack of food. And if the animals died, there would be nothing to eat.

As the weeks passed, their fears were realized. The cook fire often burned under a pot of water and peeled bark. Carrie told the children the story of Stone Soup. It made them laugh to hear about a boy who managed to get some good soup when all he had was a stone. But it didn't fill their empty bellies.

"We must return to the valley while we can," the Keeper said.

"Can you make the trip?" Sky Woman was worried. "If we stay here I will surely die," he replied. "And so will all of you."

"He is right," Swift Arrow said. "The snow will only deepen here. In the valley, it will not stay on the ground so long. We will go."

The next few days were spent in packing. Swift Arrow used two of the lodgepoles to make a kind of long sled that he called a travois. He loaded it and strapped it to Sky Woman's horse. Then he made another and piled it high with furs. He strapped it to another horse.

The Keeper's mouth settled in a straight line. "I will ride my horse," he said. "I am no woman, to be dragged behind like a sack."

Swift Arrow stood beside the horse without speaking. No one moved. The Keeper glared at him. Carrie smiled. Finally the old man settled himself on the second travois. He squirmed into the furs, grumbling all the time.

They left the summer camp in a caravan of horses. Sky Woman went first, holding Little One in front of her. Carrie's horse followed in the narrow tracks made by the travois ahead of her. Laughing Water and Small Bird, muffled in brightly striped blankets, came right behind with the other travois.

Carrie looked back at the travois but all she could see of the Keeper was a patch of grey hair and a feather. She had to laugh at the girls. They looked like tropical birds perched on the big horse that Swift Arrow had bridled for them.

At first she could not see Swift Arrow. Then a cloud of snow sprayed up some distance to the right. Swift Arrow appeared, driving the remaining horses. He rode along beside them, keeping his lance ready.

Carrie frowned at the lance. They had seen no sign of other Indians. "Maybe he does that all the time," she thought. "After all, he is a warrior."

She put her worries out of her mind. The horses plodded and plunged their way through the snowdrifts.

They rode until the trip was no longer fun. Then the girls huddled under their blankets, trying to keep warm.

The wind howled through the treetops. When Carrie turned to look back she couldn't see far. It was getting dark. The wind swept across the snowdrifts, blowing a fold of her blanket into her face. She pushed it aside.

The howling sound came again, long and wavering. Swift Arrow stopped and turned toward it. He lifted his lance. Carrie shivered. It wasn't the wind. It was some animal. And it was hungry.

Swift Arrow hurried his horse along the line of weary travelers. He stopped beside Sky Woman and pointed toward a distant ridge. She turned her horse in the direction he had pointed.

Before full dark, they reached the ridge. Swift Arrow led them through the dead underbrush to a cave in the mountainside.

They slid off the horses stiffly and turned them loose in the back of the cave. Carrie and the girls helped Sky Woman unpack the furs. Then she warmed Little One by the fire Swift Arrow had made. The child drifted off to sleep, and she tucked him into one end of the furs.

The others curled up in the furs and chewed on strips of dry pemmican. The Keeper watched Swift Arrow. The young warrior met his gaze, but neither of them spoke. After a while, Swift

Arrow wrapped himself in a bearskin and settled down next to the cave opening.

Carrie thought she was too scared to sleep, but morning came before she realized her eyes had closed. Swift Arrow was standing at the opening of the cave, looking out. Carrie got up to stand beside him. She could see nothing moving on the expanse of white in front of her. Swift Arrow moved back and kicked the fire to stir the embers.

"I'll get the firewood," Carrie said quietly.

He nodded and picked up his weapons. Carrie followed him out of the cave, walking in his footprints. When they broke dead branches off the bushes, the cracks sounded like rifle fire in the snow silence. Carrie was glad when they had enough.

They found the tracks on the way back. Swift Arrow inspected the paw prints carefully. Carrie held her breath as tightly as she held the firewood. Finally it came out in a whoosh.

"What *is* it?" she asked.

"Wolves."

Carrie gulped. "What do they want?"

Swift Arrow looked at her kindly. "Probably the horses. Small game is gone now. Come."

They hurried back to the cave. The others were up and waiting. Sky Woman built up the fire.

"We must ride," Swift Arrow said. "The valley is still three days away."

They packed and mounted the horses. Swift Arrow let them go first. He followed later, driving the horses through the snow. There was no trouble that day, nor the next. Early on the third day, Carrie thought that some of the horses were missing.

At noon they rested by a creek. Carrie watched Swift Arrow water the horses. She counted them. The piebald and the roan cavalry horse were missing.

"What happened to piebald and the roan?" she asked. "Did they run away?"

Swift Arrow shook his head. "I left them," he said. He led Sky Woman's horse back up the bank.

Carrie looked back the way they had come and shivered. Now she knew why the wolves had not followed them.

They reached the valley before nightfall. The camp stretched out along the riverbank. Melting snowdrifts tangled the long dry grass around the camp. The tipis had been placed closer together than they had during the summer. Their lodgepoles made thin black crisscrosses against the grey sky.

Smoke drifted lazily skyward. As they rode into camp, Carrie thought she had never seen anything more beautiful than the firefly glow of the cook fires.

Chapter Eight

The Challenge

Women came out of their lodges to watch them pass. They called greetings to Sky Woman. She answered cheerfully, giving no sign of her weariness. Carrie recognized White Shell, She Who Walks Crooked, and her daughter, Windsinger.

Windsinger began a song that was taken up by the other women. The song began in a trill and slurred into words. Carrie understood many of the words. She heard "daughter of the sun" and "now we will have meat in our pots."

Carrie knew that Swift Arrow was a good hunter. When he brought food home they often had shared it with the other women. The last few weeks of gnawing hunger had taught her to be thankful for his skill. But when she thought about the meaning of the song, her heart sank. Was there no food here? Would they go hungry all winter?

As she walked her horse behind Sky Woman, she looked at the drying racks outside the tipis. They were empty. She saw only a few skins of small animals. And the smells coming from the cooking pots were all too familiar. Bark and wild herbs scented the night air.

Sky Woman stopped at a bare spot. She dismounted stiffly and called to the others. Dark was coming. The tipi had to be put together quickly. Laughing Water and Small Bird and Carrie ran to help.

After the lodgepoles were cut and placed together, she helped stretch the skins around the frame. By the time the Keeper was settled inside, the need for sleep had driven her questions out of her mind. She was content to curl up inside the tipi. The tipi's closeness to other people warmed her. It no longer mattered that they were not her people.

In the morning, Small Bird and Laughing Water finished their chores early so they could play with their friends. Swift Arrow had gone to the lodge of the chief, and Sky Woman was busy outside. Carrie found herself alone with the Keeper.

Her questions from the night before flooded back. "Why did the women say they would have food now that Swift Arrow is back?" she asked. "Will it be as bad here as it was up on the mountains?"

The Keeper took his time about answering. Finally he said, "The women sang their song about you. They said their pots would be full because you were back."

Carrie was astonished. "Why?"

"Because you have the medicine bundle," he said simply.

"I don't—you mean the Bible?" Carrie's voice went up in disbelief.

"Yes." The old man shivered as wind tugged at the tipi. He settled himself deeper into the furs before he went on. "Since you came to live with us, Swift Arrow has brought home many horses. He has made many coups. He rides into battle like the wind. He cannot be killed. Others have seen it."

Carrie listened in dismay. "You don't believe that?"

The old man looked at her sadly. "No. Not anymore."

"It makes you unhappy?"

"In a way." He leaned toward her. "Some listen to your stories and hear only words. Some listen and hear only good stories."

He tapped his chest. "I listen and hope to hear the voice of the Great Spirit. Instead I hear the voice of your God. I, the Keeper of the Medicine Arrows, listen and hear."

"But that is good," Carrie said in wonder. "Why should it make you sad?"

"Because it means the beginning of the end for our tribe as it is now," the old man said. "For time before time, we have been the Cheyenne. We have followed the Buffalo Child and have seen visions we thought were sent by the Great Spirit. Now what we believe and what we are must change. But many will never believe. Some will grow angry. My sorrow is not for myself. It is for them."

"Is there anything I can do?" Carrie asked.

"Tell your stories anytime you can," the Keeper said. "They will reach a few of my people. And, told often, they will become part of our tribe's memory."

Carrie took a deep breath. She could no longer keep her secret from the old man. "I will tell them as long as I can. But I can't stay, Keeper. I have to go back to my parents."

"I know that. Perhaps it will come about in leaf-budding time." He chuckled at her surprise. "Do you think I cannot read your face? When you ask me about the stars, your eyes seek out those to the north. When you ask about tracking in the woods, you touch the moss on the north side of the tree. How could I not know?"

Carrie blushed. "Was I that clear?"

"As clear as spring rain," the old man said. "I saw. So did Sky Woman. And Swift Arrow."

"But you told me anyway." Carrie was puzzled.

"The choice to remain or go must be yours. Swift Arrow took you only by the will of your God. You will leave us the same way." He leaned back as though tired. He said her Cheyenne name, but something was different. The last syllable had changed.

Carrie fell silent. She sat quietly, thinking about what the old man said. Her mind went back to something her father had taught her long ago. "Make the most of the time and place God gives you, Carrie," he had said, "for His hand is in it." She thought for a moment, and the verse he had used came back to her.

And we know that all things work together for good to them that love God, to them who are the called according to his purpose.

Fear swept over her. "Lord, did you really send me here to be a witness for You?" she asked. "But surely I could have done as well at the mission with my parents. Why here?"

She sat and prayed until the fear left her. Then she opened her eyes and looked at the Keeper.

She thought of his kindness, his gentleness, and his understanding. She thought about leaving and knew that she would miss him. She cared for him.

After a while Carrie heard his breathing deepen. He was asleep. She arose and went outside. The fear was gone, but she felt as if she carried a huge burden on her back. Never had she felt more alone, nor more in need of her parents.

She walked down to the river. Small Bird was playing in the frozen reeds with Turtle and Pale Moon. She called for Carrie to join them. Carrie waved and turned the other way.

She looked at the warrior's trail that led through the woods back of the camp. She was tempted to take it, regardless of the weather. She knew better. Alone, she would not last one mile.

As she stood, moccasins covered with melting snow, a band of Cheyenne warriors rode down the trail. Lone Wolf and Swift Arrow rode at the front. They were empty-handed.

Lone Wolf wheeled his horse in front of Carrie. "So the daughter of the sun plays in the snow while our people go hungry," he said scornfully. "Where is your medicine now? What good does it do?"

Without waiting for a reply, he rode away. The rest of the warriors galloped with him. Swift Arrow sat on his horse and watched them go.

"You didn't find anything then?" Carrie asked.

"No." Swift Arrow held out his hand. Carrie took it. He swung her up behind him. The camp was silent as they rode into it. Women stood in groups outside their lodges. They watched the riders without speaking.

The cold Carrie felt didn't come from the winter winds. Her old fear returned. Swift Arrow stopped at their tipi. As she slid off the horse, Sky Woman hustled Carrie inside. Laughing Water, Small Bird, and Little One were already there.

"What's going on?" Carrie said quietly.

"There is trouble in the camp," Sky Woman said. "It will pass."

"But why are they mad at Daughter?" Small Bird pulled at her mother's fringes.

Sky Woman gave an exasperated sigh. "Small Bird is a magpie. She chatters too much."

Carrie took the little girl in her arms. "It's all right," she said. "I know."

She sat down next to the Keeper. He took Small Bird from her.

"You must be strong," he said to Carrie. "Soon Lone Wolf will come. You must not let him see fear. You must answer him with power."

Carrie nodded. Numbly she began to pray for wisdom and strength. When the shout came from outside, she was still without an answer.

The Keeper went to the flap. Carrie followed him outside. She saw in surprise that Swift Arrow guarded the tipi. The Keeper made a sign to him, and he stepped back.

"What do you want, Lone Wolf?" the Keeper asked the leader of the pack.

"The child you claim is from the sun," he said. "The one who has angered the Earth Mother so we have no food for the winter. The one you claim holds the words of the Great Spirit."

"I was wrong," the old man said. His voice strengthened to reach the fringe of the crowd.

A murmur began. It quieted when he lifted his hand.

"I was wrong," he repeated. "She is not the Daughter of the Sun. She is a daughter of the Son of God. She is a child of God."

Carrie recognized the change in her name. The Keeper was telling them that her God was not theirs.

Lone Wolf laughed. "Now she is a child of the Great Spirit! See how the old man builds his dreams!"

"No. I did not say Great Spirit. I said God. They are not the same." The Keeper's reply was firm.

"Then let her prove it," Lone Wolf demanded. "Let her God bring food to our people! Then we will believe!"

Carrie's mind raced. They wanted proof. A contest. The contest between Ahab and Elijah came to her. She stepped forward.

"Yes!" she said loudly. "God will provide food for you to eat. But only to prove that He is God, not to feed you!"

The crowd began to talk. The Keeper held up his hand.

"When?" asked Lone Wolf boldly.

"In the morning," Carrie said. "You will see."

The next morning, just before dawn, distant thunder woke the camp. Men, women, and children stumbled outside. Carrie stood at the entrance to the tipi and watched as a herd of deer burst from the woods.

The people stood frozen as the herd charged into the camp. Cook pots scattered and lodges tumbled under the flying hooves. Mothers snatched their children. Warriors ran for weapons as the herd passed, leaving chaos in its wake. Swift Arrow whooped and leaped on his horse. He led the band of mounted men after the deer.

Slowly Carrie let Little Bird down. She stared around at the shattered camp. Wails rose as women gathered up broken pots and trampled furs. Behind her she heard a chuckling sound.

The Keeper was laughing.

Chapter Nine

Winter Winds

The women and children spent the morning repairing the damage done to the camp. By early afternoon, snow began to drift from the thick, grey clouds that had lined the sky since dawn.

The hunters had not returned. The Keeper went to the flap of the tipi and stared toward the darkening north. Carrie joined him.

"What is it?" she asked.

"Bad snow," he said quietly. "Last for days. The men must return soon."

The rising wind whistled around the falling flakes, then moaned, then howled. The women and children sought the safety of their tipis as the icy snow slashed at the camp.

The men returned near dark. They came with heads bent against the bitter wind; their horses struggled through the blinding snow. They carried only two deer. They divided them quickly, and each man took his portion to his own tipi.

The storm lasted three days. The meat lasted less. When the snow finally stopped, the Cheyenne had to dig out of their tipis. They emerged to a white world. There was nothing that was not covered by the snow. It was as if the landscape had been painted over with a huge brush dipped in white paint. Only mounds and jagged drifts marked the places where trees and bushes stood.

After the storm, the weather cleared. A winter sun glinted off the expanse of white. Sky Woman mixed charcoal and bear grease. She rubbed the ointment under the children's eyes and across the bridges of their noses.

"It will protect you from snow blindness," she said. "For you, too," she told Swift Arrow when he entered the tipi.

He gave her a tired look and took the pot without speaking. She watched him with concern as he swept a broad mark across his face. "What's wrong?" she asked.

"Thirty, forty horses dead. Frozen."

Sky Woman bowed her head. The loss of that many horses put the tribe in danger. They needed horses for hunting, for fighting.

The Keeper struggled to a sitting position. "The bay stallion?"

"He lived. So did twenty of the mares."

"Then we'll still have a crop of spring colts." The Keeper's expression lightened.

"It won't help us now. There aren't enough horses left to mount all our warriors. We'll have to get others," Swift Arrow replied.

Carrie knew what that meant. He and a band of warriors from the tribe would go on a raid. There would be no wagon train coming through the snowbound country driving a rich remuda of loose horses. The horses would have to be taken from another tribe. Or from the army.

"Wait," the Keeper said. "The snow is too deep in the passes to drive horses. Make your raid after the spring thaw."

Swift Arrow agreed. For now, the snowbound passes would protect them from enemy attack, both from the Crow to the north and the Comanche to the south. The Keeper was right. There would be time later to get the horses.

"I will hunt this winter. Get horses later," he told his grandfather.

The deer had disappeared in the storm. All that was left in the valley was small game. And small game could be hunted on foot. Swift Arrow spent the next few days making a pair of snowshoes.

Sky Woman made snowshoes for the girls. She laced willow strips together to form the webbing between the bark frames. When she finished, the snowshoes were both light and strong.

The girls strapped them on and went outside. They no longer floundered in the snowdrifts. They walked on top. At first Carrie felt as if any minute she would plunge downward through the fluffy cloud of white. When she got used to the shuffling walk, she lifted her head and looked around.

Being so high made even familiar things look strange. The tipis were still over her head, but they no longer towered thirty feet skyward. At least eight feet of snow covered their bases. They were anchored to the frozen ground by the weight of the drifted snow.

The girls walked carefully through the camp. Everywhere Carrie went she was treated with wary respect. Even Laughing Water and Small Bird felt the pinch of the distance placed between them and the other Cheyenne. The rest of the children were playing games on the meadows. They didn't call for Laughing Water to join them.

Small Bird went off to find her friends. In a few minutes she shuffled back to Carrie, looking like a downcast raccoon. "Turtle won't play with me," she sniffled.

"He'll get over it," Carrie promised. "In a few days they will forget about everything. Then you will be friends again."

Small Bird's bottom lip thrust out. "I won't forget."

"Sure you will," Carrie said cheerfully. "If God has forgiven us, we can forgive others, can't we?"

Small Bird gave her a doubtful look. Carrie laughed. "Come; I will tell you a story of forgiveness. It's about a father and his son."

"Does he have a daughter?"

"Maybe, but she's not in the story."

The girls were always ready for Carrie's stories. They followed her to a sheltered corner and settled down to listen. Carrie raised her voice so that it would carry across the snow. Before she finished the first story, one of the younger girls came close enough to hear. Soon others came. Carrie smiled and motioned to Laughing Water and Small Bird to move over.

The women and men were not so easily won over. They spoke, but they kept their distance from Carrie. Only Lone Wolf and a few of his friends continued to give her trouble. They interrupted her stories when they could. They chased the children away. Carrie could do nothing to stop them.

The winter passed uneasily. Swift Arrow was often gone. He hunted every day, passing on what they did not need to others of the tribe. Many times Carrie found him at the tipi of the black-eyed Windsinger.

Much of everyone's time was spent in the tipis. Sky Woman kept the girls busy. Even the small hides were carefully cured and made into parts of clothing, robes, or pouches. Nothing was wasted. While Carrie worked, she talked to the Keeper.

The old man grew weaker each day. Carrie read to him often. When she could translate, she did. But he never objected to hearing the words just read, though he could not understand them.

After one bitterly cold night, Carrie woke to the sound of ragged breathing. She blinked at the yellow glow from a tallow lamp. In the shadows, she saw Sky Woman lean over the old man.

Carrie got up quietly. She knelt beside Sky Woman. "He is worse," she said.

It wasn't a question. Carrie saw the paper thin skin, the bony claws that had once been strong hands. Tears prickled behind her eyelids. She swallowed hard as the Keeper opened his eyes and looked at her.

Sky Woman stepped aside to waken Swift Arrow. The old man motioned for Carrie to come closer. "My time has come," he said faintly.

When Carrie tried to protest, he lifted one hand weakly. He gasped out the words, "I want to go as a child, not as an old man."

"A child?" Carrie was puzzled.

"A child of God. Tell me." His hand reached for hers.

Carrie bit back her tears. She didn't have to get the Bible. She knew the verses he wanted by heart.

For all have sinned, and come short of the glory of God.

But God commendeth His love toward us, in that, while we were yet sinners, Christ died for us.

The words whispered in the quiet night. The old man's grip tightened on Carrie's fingers, and

the lamplight threw shadows across the tipi. All Carrie's heart and love went into the verses.

For God so loved the world, that he gave his only begotten Son, that whosoever believeth in him should not perish, but have everlasting life.

Carrie's tears spilled over as she bent to pray with the old man. Behind her, she heard Sky Woman crying. When the Keeper finished praying, he opened his eyes. He let go of Carrie's hand.

"Swift Arrow," he said hoarsely. His hand rose shakily to point at the bundle of medicine arrows that hung from the center pole. "Cut them down."

The words came out firmly. Swift Arrow stepped back in surprise. He looked from the medicine bundle to his grandfather. The old eyes never wavered.

Slowly Swift Arrow unsheathed his knife. Obediently, he cut the cords and let the bundle of arrows fall to the ground. Sky Woman caught her breath.

The Keeper smiled. His hand fell back to the furs. His eyes closed.

Sky Woman began a long, keening death wail. Swift Arrow stopped her. "No," he said quietly. "He has chosen a different way. Let him go in peace."

He reached past Carrie and gently drew the fur robe up over his grandfather.

Two days later Carrie waited in front of the tipi. Inside, the body of the Keeper was propped upright, facing the door. All through the camp the lodgepoles of stripped tipis stretched to the sky like bare bones. Everything else was packed and ready.

Sky Woman had explained patiently that it was a great honor to move camp when a man died. And it was a special honor in winter, when it became a hardship for the tribe to move. It meant that the Keeper was an important man, a great man. Carrie looked at the lone tipi standing in the forest of poles. She still didn't like it, not one bit.

But when the chief gave the signal to move, she followed Sky Woman. The few horses were used to pull the travois. Only the smallest children rode on them. The rest of the Cheyenne wore snowshoes and walked.

At the edge of the woods Carrie stopped to look back. The wind blew through the abandoned camp, whistling around the lodgepoles. The flap of the Keeper's tipi whipped back and forth in the wind.

Carrie's throat tightened. "It's only the body," she told herself. "The Keeper is with Jesus."

Chapter Ten

One Man's Treasure

The chief led them south along the warrior's trail. He stopped a few miles downriver in an open meadow. The ground was level, the drifts few.

The people began to set up camp. By dark the center of the meadow was trampled smooth. New lodgepoles raised their spiked ends to the sky. Deer hides and buffalo skins wrapped the circle of poles to form the tipis.

Carrie helped stretch the skins around the lodgepoles Swift Arrow had cut. Their lodge was no longer located in the center of the camp.

Carrie was not disturbed. There would no longer be a fox skin of arrows hanging from their lodgepole. Swift Arrow had taken the medicine bundle to the chief. A new keeper of arrows had been chosen. The medicine bundle would hang in his lodge.

She looked around at the lodges near them. Smiling, she noticed that Swift Arrow had built the lodge close to Windsinger's. There would be a wedding in the spring.

The tipi was well built and cozy. But even packed with furs and bundles and people, it seemed empty. They all missed the Keeper. The old man's presence had filled more than his corner.

When Carrie opened her Bible to read at night, she still read the verses he liked best. Sky Woman listened as closely as the Keeper had. Carrie felt that she was trying to understand what had caused her father to turn from everything she had known as true and right.

Swift Arrow never stayed to listen. He was gone often. He had been invited to join one of the soldier societies. Carrie had hoped that he would refuse, but he didn't.

One night he did not come home at all. When he returned in the morning, he wore the strips of tanned skin, called dogstrings, that marked him as a member of the Dog Men.

Little One played with the strips of hide that dangled to the ground. Laughing Water and Small Bird giggled, awed by the change in their big brother. But Sky Woman showed no pleasure in her son. Swift Arrow frowned at Carrie and stalked out.

"What did I do?" Carrie asked.

"Nothing," Sky Woman replied. "He is angry. He thinks the Keeper turned against the Great Spirit before he died. He is afraid for us."

"Afraid?"

"Afraid that the Keeper may have been wrong. Afraid that the people will turn against us. Afraid that Windsinger will not have him if she knows. Life is full of many fears for the young," Sky Woman said. Carrie's eyes widened. She had never thought of Swift Arrow as young. He seemed so tall and strong and capable that she had never considered his age.

She thought about her father. He, too, was tall and strong and capable. She tried to imagine him afraid and could not, no more than she could imagine Swift Arrow afraid. She shook her head in puzzlement.

The winter passed more slowly than Carrie had ever thought possible. She had too much time to think. And her thoughts turned often to her parents. One night she dreamed that she took a well-kept trail leading straight north to the mission. Halfway there, the trail began to twist and turn upon itself. Weeds and thorns looped overhead. She heard the thud of running feet behind her. She awoke, thrashing in the fur covers. "It's only a dream," she whispered to herself, "It's only a dream."

She welcomed the first thunder of spring as eagerly as the rest of the tribe. She had been right about the wedding. Swift Arrow disappeared as soon as the snow in the passes thawed. He returned in a week with a string of fine horses. Most of them went to Windsinger's father. Two weeks later, Swift Arrow built a lodge for his bride.

Sky Woman stayed in her tipi with the girls and Little One. Swift Arrow still brought food for their cooking pot. But less and less often did he stay to talk.

Sometimes Carrie thought it was just as well. Some days she thought that Sky Woman would never run out of things to do. The girls seemed to have grown sticks of legs since first snowfall, and Little One was stretching the stitches in his leggings.

The deerskins Swift Arrow brought were put to use as soon as they were tanned. By the time green grass covered the ground, everyone had new clothes. This time Carrie decorated her own. She chose carefully from the small store of beads Sky Woman had saved. Then she selected perfectly straight and unbroken porcupine quills. When she finished her design, even Sky Woman smiled in approval.

The dress and leggings fit well. When Carrie ran beside the other girls, kicking the ball of buffalo hide, the dress swished around her flying legs.

She was playing one day when the ball rolled close to the woods. She ran to get it. As she bent to pick it up, a man rode down the warrior's trail. He was dressed entirely in buckskin and sported a thick black beard. He led a pack horse behind him.

His sharp eyes took in Carrie's dress, her face, and hair. But before he could say anything, he was surrounded by warriors from the camp. He held up his hands to show peace. Carrie stepped back and watched as they escorted him toward the chief's lodge.

The girls joined her, giggling and chattering. "Who is he?" Laughing Water asked.

"A brave man," one of the older girls said, "or a foolish one."

"To ride right into camp!"

The girls captured the ball from Carrie's nerveless hands and ran back to their game. Carrie walked away toward the camp. She had to see the man, talk to him.

Sky Woman met her halfway. "Come," she said impatiently. "The chief wants you in his lodge. Hurry, child!"

She took Carrie's hand and hurried her to the lodge of the chief. Outside, the stranger's horse and packhorse waited patiently. Carrie was at the flap before she realized that Sky Woman was not going in with her. She started to turn, but a quick push from Sky Woman sent her inside.

The stranger was sitting in a circle with the chief and four other warriors. In front of them lay glittering beads, knives, and boldly patterned blankets.

The chief signed to the man. "This child will speak for me and for you."

Carrie swallowed. She looked at the man. Although his hair was uncombed and his beard thick, his eyes were bright and true. He spoke first.

"Don't be afraid. Just tell them what I say," he told her.

All eyes were fixed on Carrie. She nodded.

"Tell them I need furs, many furs. Fox, beaver, wolf, buffalo, any hides."

Carrie turned and repeated his words to the chief. Then she translated the chief's reply. The conversation went back and forth between the two men. At the end, the pack was nearly empty. The chief gave a command and one of the warriors disappeared. He returned with bundles of furs, which he placed before the man. The man felt their thickness and ran his fingers through their softness. "Good," he said, looking pleased.

That night there was much dancing and singing. The man sat on a blanket beside the chief. Carrie could get no closer to him than ten feet. But over the heads of the dancers she saw him look at her.

"God will give the right time," she said to herself.

As she waited, she watched the man hungrily. Would he know her father? Would he help her?

It was near dawn before the fire burned down. Carrie sat in the shadows, her head on her chest. When the man knelt beside her, she woke instantly.

"Be ye the missionary's daughter?" the man whispered roughly. "The one that got snatched from the wagon train last summer?"

Carrie nodded. "Is my father all right? My mother? Where are they? Why didn't they come for me?"

"Scout tried to follow the trail, but the Indians were too sharp. Lost 'em right away. Wagon train waited as long as it could." The man shrugged.

"They went on to the mission?" Carrie asked. "Where is it? What direction? How could I get there?"

"Hold on, little sister," the man whispered. "It's miles across the mountains. A wee bit like yerself would never last."

"Then take me with you," she pleaded.

He shook his head. His eyes were kind. "We'd not go far that way, either. How're they treating you?"

"Fine," Carrie said. "They've been good to me."

"Then a few more weeks won't hurt." The man's voice was firm. "I'm heading south, but I'll be back. Lay low now. I'll get you back to yer folks."

As a figure approached, he stood up and stretched. The last sound Carrie heard was, "Hold on, little sister," before the man disappeared into the night.

The approaching warrior stopped in front of her. It was Lone Wolf. He looked at her and swiftly wheeled to search the night with narrow eyes. Unsatisfied, he glared down at her.

Carrie got up and turned to leave. He prowled beside her for a while. Then he too disappeared into the shadows. But all the way back to the tipi she could feel his eyes, watching, watching. She thought if she looked back, she would see them glowing yellow in the moonlight.

At Sky Woman's tipi, she fairly darted inside. Sky Woman caught her arm as she went through the flap. She pulled Carrie aside, her eyes dark with worry. "I was afraid for you," she said when Carrie looked at her in surprise. "And for me. Come."

They sat down beside the sleeping children and talked in whispers. "Will you go with him?" Sky Woman asked.

Carrie shook her head. "No. Not yet."

Sky Woman sighed in relief. "Lone Wolf watched and waited all night. You would not have gotten far."

"Why would he want to stop me?" Carrie asked. "He doesn't want me here."

Sky Woman's face was tight. "Lone Wolf never does anything without gain for himself. If he had caught you running away, he would have you, the man, and the furs. It would be a great coup for him."

Carrie shuddered. She would have fallen right into the Wolf's hands. "I wish the Keeper were here," she said. "I must get back to my family. He would help me."

"You miss them very much," said Sky Woman sadly. Her head bent. "Are they far from us?"

"They have a mission some miles from here," Carrie said. "My mother is there, and my father, my uncle and aunt, and my cousins. There are Indians there too."

"They live there?" Sky Woman lifted her head to stare at Carrie.

"Yes," Carrie replied. "My uncle and father teach them about God." She spun around impatiently, hands clasped in frustration. "If only I could get there by myself!"

"No," Sky Woman said in alarm. "You must wait. Swift Arrow will help you when the time comes."

"But he no longer comes near me," Carrie protested.

"He is torn between the old and the new," Sky Woman said. "But I know my son. He is the grandson of the Keeper. He will choose the right way."

"I have something else to tell you." Sky Woman hesitated, her face troubled. "There was much dancing. Much noise. People come and go in the night."

Carrie looked up. "What is it?"

"I have looked and looked. I cannot find it." Sky Woman wrung her hands.

"What?" Carrie swung around to look for her only treasure. Only broken thongs dangled from the thin lodgepole above her bed. The Bible was gone.

Chapter Eleven
Night Raid

Carrie was sick. She lay on her bed without moving. Her body ached and her eyes were feverish.

"I've tried everything," Sky Woman told Laughing Water. She put the bowl of herbs and water back on the fire. "Nothing works."

"Crooked Arm says she is sick because she lost her medicine," Laughing Water said. Her eyes were troubled. She sat with bent head, stroking Carrie's hair.

"He is wrong, yet he speaks true," Sky Woman said. "She is sick at heart."

"Because of the stolen Bible?"

"It tied her to her parents as surely as a rope can hobble two horses," Sky Woman replied. "Now she is truly alone."

"She has us." Laughing Water was puzzled.

"Think. She is ours, but she is not ours. If you were snatched away by a Crow, you would feel the same."

Laughing Water shuddered. She lowered her voice to a whisper. "I think Lone Wolf took the Bible."

"So do I. But his tipi was searched, just like the others. The Bible was not there. He claims the trader took it."

"The trader did not come near our tipi," Laughing Water said indignantly. "Lone Wolf lies."

They turned quickly as Swift Arrow opened the flap and stepped inside.

"How is she today?" he asked quietly.

"Not good," Sky Woman replied. "She sleeps too much."

Swift Arrow brushed them aside. "She has too much nursing. Not enough sunshine."

He picked Carrie up and shouldered his way out of the tipi. His horse was standing outside. He put Carrie on the horse and swung up beside her.

"What are you doing? Where are you going?" Sky Woman cried as he trotted away.

"I will return when the owls fly tonight," Swift Arrow said. He galloped out of the camp.

Carrie swayed back and forth in front of the young Indian. The wind whipped her hair and cooled her face. They rode in silence. Pine needles muffled the horse's hooves. Light filtered down from the green canopy of leaves. It danced over Carrie's pale skin like golden butterflies.

They left the trees and headed north over the prairie. Carrie gazed about her in wonder. The great expanse of land stretched in front of them, all the way to the sky. They rode until nothing could be seen on either side except the swaying, billowing grass.

Swift Arrow stopped. He got off the horse and handed the reins to Carrie. "Ride," he said.

Carrie stared. Slowly she took the reins. He gave the horse a sharp slap and it began to run.

Carrie leaned forward over the wind-blown mane. A sense of freedom surged through her, washed over her like the waves of sea-like grass. She rode until she was exhausted. Then she turned the horse and looked back.

There was nothing to be seen. For a moment she thought about riding on, and then shame brought a blush to her cheeks. Swift Arrow had brought her here. He had given her the freedom that woke her from her misery. She couldn't leave him on foot.

It took her an hour to find him. He was sitting in a bed of silken grass. She almost passed, but a whistle from him stopped the horse. Carrie got off to walk beside him.

"Why?" she asked simply.

"There have been times when I felt as trapped as you do," he said. "I come here and ride like the wind. It helps."

Carrie managed a smile. "Yes. It does. But how did you know I would come back for you?"

"I listen to you read. I watch. You do that which is right." He turned to look at her. "The Keeper was a wise man. He possessed all the wisdom of our tribe. Yet in death he chose your way. Why?"

"Because he knew it was the only way," Carrie said, watching his troubled face.

"But we have always believed our way is right," he said. "How can it be?"

"There is a way that seemeth right unto a man, but the end thereof are the ways of death."

The words came out before Carrie even thought them. She looked at Swift Arrow, startled.

He was not surprised. "Explain."

Carrie began to talk. Words and verses flooded back to her. They were there, a part of her.

At last Swift Arrow put her back on the horse. He got up behind her. "I will think upon your words," he said.

They reached camp by the light of a golden moon. He let her down at the tipi. "A thief may have stolen your Bible," he said, "but he could not capture the treasure that is in your heart."

Sky Woman hurried to her, clucking like a prairie hen. "What did he do? Are you all right? Come, get in bed."

Carrie gave her a hug. "No, I'm not all right. I'm wonderful. And I'm tired of bed!"

Sky Woman stared at her, round-eyed. Then she looked toward the departing horse. "The wisdom of his grandfather," she said with a satisfied smile.

Carrie took her place in camp life again. She told her stories to the children with confidence. She talked to Sky Woman, to Laughing Water, and to Small Bird. Laughing Water asked Carrie if Jesus could be in her heart too. Carrie gave her a hug and prayed with her. Sky Woman was pleased when she heard. She came to Carrie late one night.

"Will I always be afraid?" she asked.

"No," Carrie said. *"For God hath not given us the spirit of fear; but of power, and of love, and of a sound mind."*

"You are wise," Sky Woman said.

"No," Carrie replied. "God is wise."

She looked for Swift Arrow each day, for she wanted to talk again with him. But he always seemed to be busy. One day there was loud talking in the camp. Lone Wolf had gathered the warriors around him.

"There are many wagon trains crossing the land to the north," he said. "They carry guns, food, and many horses. A raid on such a train would bring us much wealth and much honor."

The young men were restless. The gusty winds of spring had stirred their blood. They had gone to the hills to seek their visions. They were ready to ride. They left at nightfall. Carrie watched them, distressed to see Swift Arrow among them. They whirled through the camp, singing and shouting. The songs of war resounded in the air. Then, in a cloud of dust, they were gone.

The camp was quiet. Carrie saw Windsinger standing alone. She was still looking in the direction the warriors had taken. Sky Woman saw her too.

"Come with us," she said kindly. "Stay with us until Swift Arrow returns."

The girl responded shyly. She came into the tipi with a quiet grace. Carrie had met her many times, but Windsinger had kept her distance. The thin girl was like a young doe, easy to startle and quick to flee.

It took a few days for the children to break past her reserve. When Carrie found her laughing with Little One and backpacking him around the tipi, she knew that Windsinger had accepted them.

The days passed slowly. Windsinger stayed at her mother's tipi, but she came to visit Sky Woman often. The women and girls worked together. Windsinger spoke to Carrie softly.

"My husband speaks well of you," she said. "He was grieved when you lost your treasure— your medicine bundle." Thoughtfully, Windsinger added, "Swift Arrow says it is not a medicine bundle like the people thought. He calls it a Bible. He tells me some of the words in it. The words have much wisdom."

Carrie smiled. So Swift Arrow had not turned aside after all. Her prayers for him would be answered. She knew it.

A few days later she was not so sure. A child ran through the camp, calling that the warriors approached. Carrie ran with Windsinger to see. Windsinger clasped her hands tightly on her chest as she saw the small number of men that rode slowly toward the camp.

They were met in silence. Some were badly wounded, hardly able to ride. Few had escaped injury. Many did not come back at all. The silence broke in a keening wail of grief that swept the camp.

"Swift Arrow," Windsinger breathed in relief. "He is here."

He rode with the first group. Carrie had not recognized him. His clothing was stained and torn. His bearing was no longer that of a proud warrior.

He and an older warrior went into the chief's tipi. When he came out, Sky Woman and Windsinger were waiting for him. They took him back to Sky Woman's tipi where Carrie waited with the children.

"When we were miles away from camp, Lone Wolf brought forth the Bible," he told Carrie.

"He said it was now his medicine. He said we would have victory."

Swift Arrow looked at Carrie with shame in his face. "I did not stop him. The desire to fight ran through my veins as strongly as it did the others. I thought as of old."

"Go on," Windsinger said gently.

"The scouts located a wagon train. We attacked. But they swung the wagons into a big circle. Their long rifles killed many of our men. Lone Wolf would not flee. Only when he was shot from his horse did we turn back."

"And the Bible?" Carrie whispered.

"Lone Wolf's horse fell near a wagon." He gestured toward his ruined clothing. "I tried to get close enough to get the bundle that contained the Bible. But I could not. I am sorry."

Carrie shook her head. "It does not matter. It was lost to me long before the raid."

Sky Woman dressed Swift Arrow's wound. Before he left, he turned again to Carrie. "I have lost that which was yours. I failed to reclaim it. To regain honor of the Keeper, I pledged to perform the Sundance. All will be put right."

Windsinger made a small sound of distress. Carrie frowned. She had never seen a Sundance since she had lived with the Cheyenne. She had heard of them. And she didn't like what she had heard.

She put a restraining hand on Swift Arrow's arm. "No," she said. "Don't do it, please. It won't help."

"I must," he said. "I have made the pledge. Now I will go into the hills to fast."

He turned to his wife. "I will return when all is ready."

Windsinger nodded. She went with him to get the things he needed.

When the flap closed behind them, Carrie turned to Sky Woman. "Why did you let him go?" she asked. "Why didn't you stop him?"

"When the arrows were stolen, the Keeper went into the hills to fast," Sky Woman told Carrie. "He, too, pledged the Sundance. It is our way."

Chapter Twelve
The Sundance

Three of the other warriors had made the same pledge that Swift Arrow had made. The date for the ceremony was set. A party of men rode ahead to ready a site on the southern bank of the river. Runners went to other camps, inviting relatives and friends to the ceremony.

The day came. The morning was spent in packing up the camp. Then the warriors took the lead, Swift Arrow in the front. Closely following the warriors were the women and children, each travois packed with camp equipment. Behind them came the youths, driving the herds of horses.

At the bank, the two lodges in which the ceremonies would take place had already been built. Moving quickly, the families took their places in the circle. In a few minutes, tipis were mushrooming on the grassy land. It seemed to Carrie that there were hundreds of them.

The women shouted greetings back and forth as they worked; the children ran in and out; the dogs yelped and fought. On the hills above the camp, bands of warriors galloped to meet newcomers, adding their own shrill yelps to the confusion.

As the tipis were completed, twilight settled on the camp. Fires crackled in the coming dark, and their smoke drifted toward the stars. By the fires, women gossiped with their friends. The children, freed from watchful eyes, ran from campfire to campfire.

After dark, the women and children gathered inside the tipis. They sat motionless, listening to the sounds outside.

Carrie caught a glimpse of a white-robed figure outside their tipi. Only dark eyes showed above the gleam of white. The figure stood still for a moment in the light of the moon. Then other figures joined it, and they moved away from the tipi.

"What's going on?" Carrie whispered to Sky Woman.

"The men gather," was her answer. "They dress in white. No one knows the one who walks beside him. Only if the person speaks can he be recognized. They all go to the ceremonial lodge."

"What do they do there?" Carrie persisted.

"A woman does not know," Sky Woman replied. "Sleep now."

Carrie lay down, but she did not sleep. The air was charged with a strange excitement. Holiday excitement at home had always made her happy and full of anticipation. But this excitement left her troubled and full of dread.

The next day was a day of visiting for the women. Sky Woman took Carrie with her. Again Carrie was subjected to probing curiosity. She was surprised that some of the women had heard of her.

"The Storyteller," they called her. Carrie liked that name much better than she had liked Daughter of the Sun. When they asked for stories, Sky Woman was pleased. She sent the children to play while Carrie began to tell one of Sky Woman's favorites.

The women came and went, but always there was a clamor for more stories. By the time the day was over, Carrie's voice was hoarse.

The next day, the old men chose the centerpole for the sunlodge. The lodge would be huge, big enough to hold many people during the dance. The young men traveled miles to cut lodgepoles from a stand of cottonwood. They draped their horses in branches and leaves so thick that the horses were almost hidden. Then they roped the shorn pole and galloped back to the camp.

It was during the preparation for the lodge that the trapper came. He had sold the furs and returned with a bulging pack to bargain for more.

In the spirit of celebration, he was welcomed into the camp. He rode in the midst of a band of young warriors, paying no heed to their shrill yelps and yells. He passed Carrie without turning his head; yet she felt sure that he had seen her.

Carrie turned to see Sky Woman watching her. Sky Woman dropped a ladle back into the buffalo stew and hurried inside the tipi. Concerned, Carrie followed.

"What is it?" she asked.

Sky Woman bent her head. "I have grown used to your presence," she said. "You are like my own daughters."

Carrie hugged her Indian mother. "I love you too," she said. The words came out in a rush. "You and Laughing Water and Small Bird and Little One. And Swift Arrow and Windsinger."

Sky Woman wiped her eyes. "I am sorry. I should rejoice that your time has come. You must go."

Carrie shook her head, caught between excitement and sorrow. "We don't know that. Last time, the trapper could not take me."

"It is different now. The people know that your Bible was not medicine like the medicine arrows. They know that you do not come from the Great Spirit. Lone Wolf is not here to seek revenge or glory. It is time for you to go."

Carrie didn't reply. She thought about the roving bands of warriors on the hills. They guarded the camp and welcomed latecomers to the Sundance. That way was closed. How would they get away? What if she were caught again?

Carrie was not called to the chief's lodge. No business would be conducted until after the ceremony. The trapper was free to move within the camp. Carrie saw him often during the day; but he moved past her as if she were only one of the Indian girls.

She was puzzled at his attitude of indifference. She thought that perhaps he had changed his mind and had decided not to help her. After all, if he did, he would no longer be welcome to trade in the lodges of the Cheyenne.

Early in the afternoon the people gathered in the center of the circle. Expectantly they looked toward the first lodge. The drum began to throb.

A painted woman emerged from the lodge. She wore a buffalo hide, fur side out. She walked bent over, close to the ground. She carried a stuffed buffalo skull. Tufts of sage decorated her hair and her wrists. Carrie's heart sank when she recognized Windsinger.

Behind her came the old men, followed by Swift Arrow and the other pledgers. They were painted in white stripes running down from head to foot. Carrie felt like she was looking at strangers.

The procession stopped, and Windsinger sat down, the buffalo skull in front of her. Carrie stepped aside as women and children surged past her to be blessed by the pledger's wife.

Beside her, Sky Woman caught Small Bird's hand to keep her from rushing forward. They watched the rest of the ceremony in silence. Carrie glanced across the crowd of milling women. She saw the trapper, standing with the chief. His arms were folded. He, too, watched the ceremony in silence.

Twilight came and the centerpole was raised into place. The rafters and lodgepoles followed, and the sides were stretched with lodge-covers. Windsinger stood up. With the others, she entered the sunlodge.

A swarm of people swept past Carrie on their way into the sunlodge. Some rode their horses in, shouting loudly and shooting into the top of the centerpole.

Finally the noise dwindled and along with it, the crowd. Only the pledgers and Windsinger remained in the lodge.

After dark, the drum began again. This time Carrie did not leave the tipi. Sky Woman stayed with her. So did the children.

"He is your son," Carrie said. "You must go."

"I have been to Sundances many times," Sky Woman said. "Most men dance to the drums until they drop from exhaustion. I have only seen one man dance against the thongs. That was my father."

"Then why is Swift Arrow doing it?" Carrie asked. "If it isn't done that much, why?"

"Because he blames himself for what has happened," Sky Woman said. "Just as his grandfather did. And I am afraid that he is pledging himself to our customs. He has made his choice."

Carrie's heart sank. "But he listened. He cared. I could tell that God was working in his heart."

"But as you once told us," Sky Woman said slowly, "the decision is his. He must will it."

Carrie nodded. "What about Windsinger?"

"She will follow her husband. His choice will be her choice."

Disappointment made Carrie restless. She paced back and forth to the beat of the drums. "How long will it go on?" she asked.

"Three, four sunrises."

Carrie barely slept that night. Long after the drums were silent, she heard them in her mind. She got up and walked outside. Above the camp the stars sparkled as brightly as before. For some reason she had felt that they would be dimmed by what had gone on tonight.

Their brightness reassured her. Her heart lightened. Nothing that went on here could dim God's greatness, nor lessen His power.

Four days later the ceremony was finished. Carrie watched as Windsinger led Swift Arrow away to rest. He didn't look like the young warrior who had saved her life on more than one occasion. The white stripes had blurred in the heat of the dance. Dried blood caked on the strips of flesh torn from his chest.

Around her, women began to pack in preparation for the return trip to their own camps. Sky Woman had begun to strip their tipi when a man came for Carrie. Sky Woman stopped her work and went with her.

The warriors and old men had gathered in the circle around the chief's tipi. The trapper sat beside the chief. His wares were spread out on a piece of canvas in front of them. The Sundance was over. It was time for business.

The men bartered all morning. In the end, many furs lay beside the trapper. The canvas pack was nearly empty. The crowd began to drift away.

Carrie stood up to go.

"Wait," the trapper told her. He took a smaller, carefully wrapped package from his horse. He unrolled it in front of the chief. Inside were blankets finer than those he had just traded, a well-made pipe, several knives, and a separately wrapped article.

The trapper let the chief inspect the package. He refused the chief's first offer. And the second. The chief persisted. "What do you wish?"

"The girl here," said the trapper. "I wish her freedom."

Carrie stared at the trapper. Then she turned to face the chief. His face was calm and undisturbed.

He showed no interest. "Three furs," he said.

The trapper unwrapped the last item. He held it so Carrie could not see. The chief stood up quickly. He motioned to the new Keeper and took the package inside the tipi.

"What *was* it?" Carrie asked, startled.

"One of the medicine arrows stolen from the tribe," the trapper said, eyes twinkling. "Traded it from a Crow."

Behind them, Sky Woman caught her breath. Carrie looked at her. Her eyes were shining. "It will work," she whispered to Carrie.

The chief and old men came out, excitement in their bearing. "We will trade the girl," the chief said. "But we must speak to Swift Arrow."

They sat down to await the young warrior. He came, wrapped in a blanket. He listened without speaking as the chief spoke. He watched Carrie's face.

"Yes," he said. "I give my permission."

"My son." Sky Woman stood up. She held out her hand toward Swift Arrow. "I wish to go with the girl."

Swift Arrow stared at her. Sky Woman held her head high. She did not flinch as she met his eyes.

"She is my daughter. I have accepted her God. I wish to go with her."

"What about Laughing Water, Small Bird, Little One?" he asked angrily.

"They will go with me. You are married now. You will have a family of your own. You have made your choice, as my father and I made ours. Let us go."

The chief fingered the rewrapped medicine arrow. He looked at Swift Arrow.

Finally the young man nodded. "You may go," he said, and turned away.

Chapter Thirteen
The North Star

The last of the stragglers were still moving out of the camp as Sky Woman and Carrie finished packing. Carrie was trembling with excitement. She fished Little One out of the travois for what she hoped was the last time.

"Laughing Water," she shouted. "Come and watch this boy!"

When the girls hurried to take the child, she warned them nervously, "Don't go far. Don't get lost."

"We won't get lost here." Laughing Water smiled. She had never seen Carrie so flustered. "Tell me again where we go."

"To the north," Carrie said, her eyes alight. "We'll travel the Oregon Trail for a while. Then we'll take a cutoff to the mission. My father is there, and my mother is there. And my aunt and uncle and cousins!"

"Will they like us?" Small Bird's voice was serious.

"Yes, yes," Carrie said, giving her a quick kiss. "They'll love you."

The trapper was ready. They joined him at the chief's lodge. He looked at their travois and equipment, and then he sighed. "Just what I wanted," he groaned, "to travel across Injun territory with a passel of women and cooking pots!"

Everyone gathered to see them off. Swift Arrow was there. So was Windsinger. She hugged Little One tightly with tears in her eyes. "I won't forget you," she said to Carrie. "Ever."

Swift Arrow was no longer angry. He told his family goodbye and turned to Carrie. "Go in peace, sister," he said to her. "Someday we will talk again."

"Come to the mission," Carrie said tearfully. "You will be welcome there."

"Time's awastin'," said the trapper. He started out, expecting them to follow. They fell into their old pattern: Sky Woman and Little One first, Carrie next, and the girls last.

Carrie kept her place though she had a million questions she wanted to ask the trapper. She forced them back and kept riding. At night they made camp under a clump of cottonwoods at the river.

"How much farther?" she asked the trapper.

"Two weeks, maybe more to the mission," he said. "Hard to tell. Have to cross bad country. Injuns up north been raising dust for a while."

"Raising dust?"

"Some renegade Cheyenne's been stirring them up. Formed his own band. Been raiding wagon trains up in the mountains."

"What's his name?" she asked.

"The renegade?" The trapper hobbled his horse. "Wolf Scar. Got a saber cut across his face."

Carrie let out her breath in relief. Her heart had jolted at the name of Wolf. She gave herself a mental shake. Lone Wolf was dead. Dead and gone.

She hurried to help Sky Woman. They cooked, then quickly doused the fire. The trapper watched the children constantly to make sure they didn't wander out of sight.

Carrie caught his nervousness. Sky Woman brought the children back to camp. The next night they didn't make camp. They ate dried pemmican and slept under the stars. Carrie and Sky Woman picked up the trapper's caution. They watched the trail. The girls rode close together.

They followed the North Star. Carrie thought of the Keeper and the time they had studied the stars together. She found herself looking at moss on the trees and signs along the trail. She smiled, remembering.

A week later they reached the worn trail left by the wagons. It showed no sign of travel within the last week or so. They followed the trail up into the mountains.

They saw the raiding party on the fifth day. The trapper motioned for silence. He led them off the trail, into the brush. They traveled slowly through the rocky hills, keeping out of sight.

"Do you think they saw us?" Carrie asked.

"Too far away," was the curt reply. The trapper shook his head in disgust. "Sure to find our tracks though. 'Bout here's where I usually cut and run."

"Maybe they won't see our trail," Carrie suggested hopefully.

"Not likely." The trapper shook his head. "Just pray they run into a well-loaded wagon train."

"I can't do that!" Carrie was shocked.

"Well, little sister," he said, "if they don't, we might as well dig in right now. Speakin' of which, there's a cave up yonder a bit. Might make a good stand-off place."

"Could we hold them off long?" Carrie asked.

"Depends on who's got the most ammo, us or them," he replied. "Tho' odds might be in our favor. Long knives patrol this area ofttimes. Might run into them."

"Long knives?"

"Cavalry. Horse soldiers," he said. "Since the raids, the forts send out patrols now and then to try to keep the peace. Or ketch the murderin' devils."

He led them up a steep, rocky trail. At the top was a deep-set cave. Its mouth was protected by an overhanging ledge and steep, sloping sides. The only access was the trail to its mouth.

The cave echoed as they led the horses inside. The trapper inspected it carefully. He grunted in satisfaction. "Tight as a fort," he said. "We'll hole up here for a spell."

"What about water?" Sky Woman said. "We must have water to drink."

"All the comforts of home," he said more cheerfully. "Running water in the back."

Carrie filled their jugs from the spring and watered the horses. Sky Woman prepared a cold supper. Small Bird's bottom lip trembled when she saw the food, but she didn't complain.

Several days passed without incident. The trapper grew restless. He paced back and forth in the mouth of the cave. Finally he got his rifle.

"You stay here," he told the women. "I'm going to scout around.

Carrie nodded. She watched as he made his way down the trail. He was halfway down when she saw a movement from behind one of the rocks. Then an Indian stood up and drew back on his bow. It was Lone Wolf.

Carrie's scream echoed in the canyon. The trapper flattened himself behind a rock. The arrow glanced off the rock a second later. The Indian disappeared.

The trapper worked himself back up the trail under a hail of arrows. Most were too far away to do more than bounce harmlessly off the rocks. He scrambled frantically back into the cave.

"Thanks, gal," he said breathlessly. "It almost got me that time."

"It was Lone Wolf," Carrie said hysterically.

"No, no," Sky Woman said, trying to calm her. "Lone Wolf is dead. He is dead."

"No, he isn't." Carrie shook her head violently. "He has a scar across his face from his left eye to his chin. But it was him. He is alive."

"It is not possible. Swift Arrow saw him fall at the wagon train," Sky Woman said.

"Don't mean much." The trapper wasn't surprised. "Could have wriggled away through the grass, using the battle as cover. Wouldn't put anything past that snake."

"But why didn't he come back?" Sky Woman asked.

"Who led the raid?" the trapper asked in return.

"Lone Wolf," was the reply.

"Probably lost face. If he had come back, would he have been welcome?"

"No," Sky Woman said slowly. "We lost many men. We gained nothing."

"There's yer answer. Most bullies are cowards at heart," he said. "Didn't want to face up to his own medicine."

An arrow glanced off the side of the cave. He stepped back, waving the women deeper into the cave. "Don't reckon either of you can shoot?" he asked.

When they shook their heads, he sighed loudly. "Figured."

He had two guns. Carrie kept one loaded as he fired the other. The Indians backed down the trail under the deadly rifle fire.

"What now?" Carrie asked.

"Pray," said the man.

"I have been," Carrie replied. "So has Sky Woman."

The trapper gave her a look of surprise. "The Indian woman?"

"Yes," Carrie replied firmly. "She's a Christian."

The trapper shrugged. "She's Cheyenne. If this here's one of her tribe, maybe she can talk to him. Get him to back off."

"Maybe," Carrie said doubtfully. "I guess it couldn't get worse."

Sky Woman went to the mouth of the cave. "Lone Wolf!" she called. "It is I, Sky Woman."

From far below came an answering hail.

"Why do you fight against your own?" she called.

"I want the girl," he called back. "Give her to me. Then you can go free."

Carrie blinked. "He *did* see us!"

"No," Sky Woman shouted. "She is my daughter. Go on your way!"

Lone Wolf's answer flew from his bow. The arrow curved upward and splintered on the rocks. "Die then!"

"Has it in for ye," the trapper observed. "What'd you do to him?"

"She did nothing," Sky Woman said indignantly. "Lone Wolf made his own mistakes out of greed and envy. He failed in everything he tried to do."

"Well, he's got us over a barrel," the trapper observed. "Unless there is a patrol nearby that heard those shots of mine."

"Is that likely?" Carrie asked.

"Maybe," the trapper replied. "They come out at different times. To fool the Injuns, ye see. But if a patrol is in the area at all, they'll hear it. A Sharps rifle carries a long way."

"Then we'll trust that they're on the way," Carrie said firmly. "Small Bird, Laughing Water, let's have a hot supper."

The trapper gave her an incredulous look, then burst into laughter. "Wall, I guess hot's fine

enough. We don't have to worry about being seen, do we?"

A hot supper left them all feeling better. After they finished, Carrie led Sky Woman and the girls in prayer while the trapper kept watch.

She felt his surprised glance. But when she looked up, he was intently watching the line of Indians scrambling up the trail. He drew a bead on one and squeezed the trigger. The Sharps boomed, then the revolver. The sound echoed in the cave.

When Carrie heard the bugle, she thought her ears were still ringing from the echo. Then the sound came again, clear as a bell. Below them the Indians scrambled to get back down the trail. They ran straight into the cavalry that poured into the canyon.

"Ye did it, gal!" the trapper whooped. "Ye did it. Ye prayed 'em through!"

Chapter Fourteen

Home

The trapper made them wait until one of the troopers came to get them. "Can't be too cautious," he said. "Had a friend once who stuck his head out too soon. One Injun hadn't given up."

Carrie came to stand beside him. She watched the activity below. It looked like most of the Indians had been captured. "Do you think they got Lone Wolf?"

"Maybe," the trapper said. He scratched his beard. He pointed at an approaching figure. "We'll find out soon enough."

The trooper stopped halfway. "Hallo, the cave," he called. "Need help?"

"Naw," the trapper bellowed back. "We're on our way down."

Sky Woman and Carrie harnessed the horses and led them out. The small party picked its way down the rocky trail. It was harder going down than it had been going up.

At a particularly bad spot Carrie thought the bay mare was going to slide down on top of her. Ahead of her, Little One clung to his mother's back. The travois slid, spooking her horse.

The trooper scrambled up the last few feet. He grabbed the horse as Sky Woman stumbled. She caught hold of a large rock to steady herself. The trooper led the horse on down.

At the bottom of the cliff, the officer in charge waited for them. "Anyone hurt?"

"We're right as rain," the trapper replied, "thanks to little sister here."

The lieutenant turned to Carrie. His eyes widened. "Would you by any chance be Caroline Talbot?" he asked.

"Yes," she said eagerly. "How did you know?"

He took off his hat. "Can't imagine many redheaded girls running around in buckskin dresses," he replied with a grin. "We've been looking for you."

"Took your time, didn't ye?" The trapper grunted in disgust. "Had to rescue the lady myself. Ransomed her. Cost me plenty, too."

The lieutenant ignored him. "We lost the trail when you were first taken. Gave you up for good until we found the Bible."

Carrie took a deep breath. "You found it!"

"Yes," he replied. "The buckskin cover had protected it well. The Bible inside was perhaps a little stained, but still in good shape."

"How did you find it?" Carrie asked quietly.

"We found it after a raid on a wagon train," he said. "It was tied on a dead horse."

"Lone Wolf's horse," Carrie said. "He stole it and took it on that raid. He thought it would bring him good medicine."

"Lone Wolf?" The lieutenant was puzzled.

Carrie looked toward the prisoners. "Him," she said, pointing to Wolf Scar. "He is the one."

Lone Wolf spat and turned his back on her. Carrie didn't care. She was well and safe, and her Bible was safe, too.

"I see," said the lieutenant.

"How did you know little sister was still alive then?" asked the trapper. "The Injun could've killed her."

"We didn't," he replied. "But a Sioux at Ft. Laramie recognized the Bible. He told us we might find the girl in a Cheyenne camp. We've been checking them all. Last one told us of a girl called Storyteller who lived with the Cheyenne on Bitter Creek. We were headed there."

"What about my parents," Carrie said eagerly. "Are they all right?"

"We sent word to them about finding the Bible. They're coming to pick it up at Ft. Laramie." He slapped the dust out of his gloves and put his hat on his head. "Matter of fact, if we get cracking, we might catch them before they come and go. Come on."

"Not me," said the trapper. "I got business up river."

Carrie took his hand. "But I want you to meet my folks. You saved my life. They'll want to thank you."

"I didn't do it fer thanks," he said. He cleared his throat. "Don't need any. You go along now, little sister."

"Then come to see us at the mission," Carrie pleaded.

"Might." The trapper kicked his horse into a trot. He yelled back, "Never can tell!"

Carrie joined the line of soldiers. The lieutenant brought her and the others up front so the dust wouldn't blow into their faces. Carrie talked to him as she rode.

He answered questions until the fort appeared in the distance. Then Carrie fell silent. All her attention was focused on the fort and the people within its walls.

When they entered its opened gates, Carrie was a mass of nerves. Her first impression was of nothing but horses and soldiers and wagons. Then people emerged into her line of sight—men, women, and children from the wagon trains. They stopped to watch the line of soldiers approach.

Murmurs arose from the crowd as they saw Carrie's fiery hair.

"It's a white girl!"

"She's wearing Injun clothes, Ma!"

"Poor thing, reckon she was captured. Probably lost her folks."

Carrie blocked their voices out. She scanned the quadrangle quickly. Her gaze caught a tall, broad-shouldered man as he stepped from a shadowy room. The man held out his hand to a lady as she stepped down onto the boardwalk. The woman held a fringed buckskin bundle in her hand.

Carrie's heart thudded hard against her chest. Her throat closed up. The man turned toward them just as the woman looked up. Her hand went to her throat, and her eyes opened wide. Carrie saw her mouth move, but she could not hear the words.

"Ma! Pa!" Carrie was off the horse before it stopped. She met her parents more than halfway. She hugged them both at the same time, laughing and crying all at once.

It took some time before she remembered Sky Woman and the children. When she did, she hurried back. "Come," she told Sky Woman. "You must meet my mother."

Sky Woman followed her shyly. The two girls stayed close to the fringes on her skirt. Little One swaggered along behind, imitating the rolling walk of the sergeant.

Martha and Nathan Talbot welcomed them warmly. They drew the Indian woman and children into their circle of family as if they had been next-door neighbors. Sky Woman relaxed. Soon she and Martha Talbot were chattering like old friends.

"Ma," Carrie said wonderingly. "You speak Cheyenne as well as I do!"

"You forget that we have a mission," her father said. "Many of the Northern Cheyenne come to our mission. We learn as many dialects as we can to reach the people for Christ. If we can't speak the language, we use an interpreter. Failing that, sign language."

Martha hugged Carrie again. "Just think, if the Bible had not been found . . ."

"I had it with me most of the time," Carrie told her. "Sky Woman made the cover to protect it."

"Yes," Sky Woman said. "We listen to the words. We believe."

Carrie's father turned to her. "But how?"

Carrie recited a verse in Cheyenne. "See, I had to learn too, Pa. First for the Keeper, then for the others."

"How wondrous are the ways of the Lord," her mother marveled.

In her joy, all hardships were erased from Carrie's mind. They returned to the mission rejoicing. The welcome they received there kept Carrie on a cloud of happiness. Only later, when she had grown more accustomed to her new life, did she think of Swift Arrow.

She went in search of Sky Woman. She found her helping Aunt Julie with the Indian children's Bible study. She looked up and saw Carrie in the doorway of the log hut. Smiling, she left the children and came to talk to her.

"You frown, my daughter," she said, touching Carrie's forehead. "I have not seen such crooked lines since we came here to stay. What troubles you?"

"I was thinking of Swift Arrow," Carrie replied, "and Windsinger. Will we never see them again?"

Sky Woman was silent a moment. "The words of your mother stay with me. She said the ways of the Lord are wondrous. He sent you to us. Perhaps he means for Swift Arrow to stay with the tribe. I am sure he will be chief someday."

"But—"

Sky Woman touched Carrie's lips. "And if he is chief, he will be able to lead his people."

Light dawned in Carrie's eyes. "You mean, if he accepts Christ, he can lead the others."

"Yes, it is for that I pray," Sky Woman said. She turned to look back at the children. Laughing Water looked up and waved happily. "And for their children."

Carrie's frown was gone. "Then so will I, Sky Woman."

She started away, then ran back to hug the Cheyenne woman. "I gained one other blessing this year," she said warmly. "I have two mothers."

She went back to the house, where Martha Talbot had started preparing the noon meal. She washed her hands at the back door. But before she went to work, she stopped to look into the front room. Her father was preaching to a group of warriors, both young and old. Her eyes were drawn to the big book he held in his hands. On the table beside him lay the buckskin cover.

He was preaching about laying up treasure in heaven. Carrie listened for a minute. She smiled as she heard the words that had sustained her through a whole year alone:

". . . for where your treasure is, there will your heart be also."

Author's Note

Before the first wagon train crossed the prairie in 1841, Indian raids were directed against neighboring tribes. Most tribes did not fight to acquire new territory, but they were quick to defend what they considered their own hunting grounds. They raided other tribes for horses and captives. They fought for revenge and to demonstrate their bravery in battle. *Counting coup* (touching a live enemy in battle and living to tell about it) was considered braver than actually taking a life.

By the time our story begins in 1853, the trails west were well worn, and peace had become more difficult to maintain. Hostile acts were more frequent on the part of both whites and Indians. A year after Carrie Talbot returned to her parents, the Plains Wars began. The Cheyenne, as a people, kept the peace longer than more aggressive tribes. But incidents still occurred, and misunderstandings developed on both sides. Ten years later, in 1864, the Chivington Massacre wiped out a peaceful Cheyenne camp at Sand Lake. The Cheyenne entered the Plains Wars with a vengeance. Events on both sides were brutal. When the wars ended in 1890, the tribes were settled on reservations. In the span of fifty years, the day of the freely roaming Plains Indian was finished.